THE *TITANIC* LOCKET

THE HAUNTED MUSEUM

THE *TITANIC* LOCKET

BOOK ONE

Suzanne Weyn

SCHOLASTIC INC.

ISBN 978-0-545-58842-3

12 11 10 9 8 7 6 5 4 3   14 15 16 17 18/0

Printed in the U.S.A.   40
First printing, October 2013

The text type was set in Old Style 7.
Book design by Abby Kuperstock

For my terrific readers. You rock!

THE *TITANIC* LOCKET

INTRODUCTION

WELCOME. You have arrived at the Haunted Museum. It's a place where dreams are made — bad dreams! Ghostly phantasms float. When you least expect it, a hand grabs your throat. A jar falls and unleashes an ancient curse.

I opened the Haunted Museum many, *many* years ago. And I've been adding to its special displays for longer than I can recall.

Some say the museum has become a worldwide

chain — just an entertaining fraud for the amusement of tourists.

Others see something more mysterious, more
sinister within its walls.

Either way, no one escapes unaffected by what
they find within the museum. The items that touch
your hands will come back to touch your life in a
most terrifying manner.

Take, for instance, the case of two sisters,
Samantha and Jessica Burnett, who are about to
embark on a cruise into a ghostly past thanks to a
peculiar locket they first see at . . . the Haunted
Museum.

Happy Haunting,

Belladonna Bloodstone

Founder and Head Curator

THE HAUNTED MUSEUM

I CAN'T BELIEVE we just arrived in England and we're leaving already," twelve-year-old Samantha Burnett grumbled as she and her sister, Jessica, only eighteen months older, wandered the darkened halls of the Haunted Museum.

Their parents had booked the family on a cruise liner during the girls' spring break from school. The *Titanic 2* was a replica of the original *Titanic*, from the four huge funnels to the famous grand staircase. The Burnetts had come to England just so they could board at Southampton, the port from which the first *Titanic* had sailed in April 1912. This cruise would follow the exact route the *Titanic* had charted from England to America, with stops in France and Ireland.

With time to kill before their departure, Jessica had insisted on seeing the nearby Haunted Museum, located a block from the ship. "This brochure says they have a special *Titanic* exhibit. It will be educational. Maybe we'll learn something cool about the *Titanic*."

The word *educational* had worked its magic with their parents and they'd given their permission. "Be ready to leave as soon as I text you, though," Mrs. Burnett insisted. "I don't want to miss the boat!"

"We will," Jessica had agreed.

Samantha had never been in a Haunted Museum before. But so far her impression was that it was a sort of cross between Madame Tussauds wax museum, Ripley's Believe It or Not!, and The Haunted Mansion at Disney. In the front entrance hall alone, they'd seen a motion-activated talking skeleton dressed to be the pirate Long John Silver, a moldering mummy who bolted into a sitting position from his sarcophagus, the ax supposedly used by the infamous Lizzie Borden in 1892, and the alien who purportedly crashed in Roswell, New Mexico, back in 1947.

Deeper inside they came to a table featuring an amulet of a beetle encased in amber. "Wouldn't that be cool to wear?" Jessica commented as the sisters stared down at it. She reached forward to touch it.

A female guard dressed all in black stepped abruptly out of the corner. "Please don't touch!"

Startled, the girls clasped each other's arms.

The woman pointed to the sign over the doorway. It was lit from behind by a small bulb.

DO NOT TOUCH ANY DISPLAY.

She then pointed to two more of the exact same signs arranged around the room.

"We get the point," Jessica whispered to Samantha as they nodded.

"See that you do," the guard insisted firmly.

The girls moved away quietly. "How did she even hear that?" Jessica whispered.

Samantha shrugged. "She gave me the creeps. Let's leave."

Jessica grabbed the sleeve of Samantha's cotton sweater. "But there's still forty minutes till we need to head back. Look, here's the *Titanic* exhibit. Come on."

Life-size mannequins, dressed in the fashions of 1912 — the year the cruise ship *Titanic* sank —

stood in glass cases lit from within. Samantha read the names of the different figures: Molly Brown, American, philanthropist (saved); Benjamin Guggenheim, American, millionaire (drowned); W. T. Stead, British, journalist and publisher (drowned); Mr. and Mrs. Isidor Strauss, American, owners of Macy's department store (drowned). Samantha stood back, taking in the apparel each mannequin wore: Molly Brown's wide, feather-brimmed bonnet and parasol; Benjamin Guggenheim's long-tailed jacket and ankle-high, buttoned boots; the pinned ascot worn by W. T. Stead; Mrs. Strauss's beautiful print shawl and her husband's rounded, black bowler hat.

"Look at this, Sam!" Jessica called, waving Samantha over to one of the life-size figures: a well-dressed man walking a dog with tightly curled fur. He wore a flat straw hat with a round brim and smoked a pipe.

Samantha brushed aside her dark bangs as she stooped to study the model of the Airedale terrier straining at the leash. "It looks so real." She smiled up at her sister. "Cute dog, isn't it?"

Jessica nodded. "This is John Jacob Astor," she read from the information card glued to the case. "He was an American billionaire who went down with the *Titanic*."

"And the dog is named Kitty!" Samantha read over her sister's shoulder. "Oh, that's funny."

"It says here that John Jacob Astor opened up all the kennels before the ship sank so that the dogs would have a chance to survive," Jessica continued. "No one is really sure if that's true or not, though."

Samantha thought about it a moment. "I hope it's true. That was a nice thing to do."

"I know you love animals," Jessica commented, smiling.

Samantha gazed at their reflections in the case's glass. Here in the low light she could see why people sometimes mistook her and her sister for twins. But Jessica was the outgoing one with the dazzling smile and quick laugh. Samantha was also friendly but didn't quite make the same big impression as Jessica.

"See how our reflections are hovering right next to Astor?" Jessica noted. "We look like ghosts!"

"He's the ghost, not us," Samantha objected. Something about Jessica's words had caused gooseflesh to rise on her skin. Maybe it was just the too-cold air-conditioning.

They continued on into another room and examined objects that had been salvaged from the sunken ship: eight hundred cases of shelled walnuts; five grand pianos; a fifty-phone switchboard; an ice machine from C Deck; a Model T Ford; sixteen trunks marked with their owner's name,

Ryerson; a cask of china dishes; a case of gloves from the Marshall Field's department store.

"How big was this ship?" Samantha asked as she perused the seemingly endless collection.

"Huge," Jessica answered. She was intently studying a case filled with jewelry that had gone down with the ship: diamond necklaces; sparkling ruby brooches; an emerald bracelet; gold earrings of various designs, including a drop pearl that shone moon-white.

"That's a lot of bling," Samantha commented as she came to Jessica's side.

"Look at this silver locket. Isn't it beautiful?" Jessica remarked. Samantha looked to where Jessica pointed at a table displaying the less valuable jewelry. The locket was closed and etched with a lily design. "I'm dying to know whose pictures are inside," Jessica went on, still focused on the locket.

Looking quickly from side to side, she snatched the locket from the display.

"Jess!" Samantha hissed under her breath. "Don't!"

"I just want to see what's inside."

"We'll get into trouble," Samantha insisted.

In a flash, Jessica pried the locket open. Samantha peered over her sister's shoulder to see. The pictures on either side were faded and chipped beyond recognition. "I bet the water did this," Jessica whispered.

Samantha spied a figure moving across the room toward them. It was the woman guard who had scolded them before.

"Put it back," Samantha urged her. "Quick."

"I can't."

"What do you mean?" Samantha asked in a nervous whisper.

A look of alarm shot across Jessica's face. "I can't open my hand."

The woman was getting closer. She was definitely heading for them. Seized with panic, Samantha slapped Jessica's hand hard.

The locket fell, open, back onto the display table.

With a lightning movement, Samantha shut the halves closed. "Let's get out of here," she insisted, pulling Jessica with her through the first door she found.

. . .

Samantha kept one anxious eye on the door of the gift shop they'd hurried into. Was the woman coming in to scold them for touching the locket? The Haunted Museum seemed pretty serious about their *no touching* rule. Even the gift shop had signs that said: YOU BREAK IT, YOU'VE BOUGHT IT and DON'T TOUCH UNLESS YOU INTEND TO BUY.

The woman guard appeared in the doorway. Her eyes darted around the shop.

She was searching for them! Samantha was sure of it. Grabbing Jessica by the hem of her T-shirt, she pulled her behind a high display of plastic swords, replicas of those used by the murderous Attila the Hun and his marauding army. "We're going to get caught. Why did you have to touch that locket?"

"I wanted to see what was inside," Jessica defended herself. "You touched it, too."

"Just to close it!"

"Well, she's not looking for us," Jessica insisted, peering above the sword display. The sisters kept low as they tracked the guard's movements from their hiding place. It seemed like she was looking for *something*. They both heaved a sigh of relief when the guard left by a side entrance.

"I told you there was nothing to worry about," Jessica said, stepping out from behind the sword display.

"Let's get out of here before she comes back," Samantha said urgently.

"She won't," Jessica scoffed confidently. "She's already decided we're not in here."

"I hope so. Let's go."

"Not yet. I want to see what they have in the gift shop."

Samantha sighed, not even bothering to argue. Jessica was crazy about gift shops, and Samantha knew they'd be there for at least another twenty minutes. She decided to make the best of it and look around. She was admiring a counter displaying stuffed Airedale puppies when her phone vibrated.

A quick check revealed that she had a text from her mother.

> We're waiting outside. Ship is leaving
> soon. Please hurry.

Turning in a circle, Samantha located Jessica at a counter across the gift shop. "Come on. We have to go. Mom just texted me. The ship is leaving."

Samantha's phone buzzed again. This time she didn't even bother to check it. "Come on. If we miss the ship, Mom and Dad will ground us for life. You know how they hate it when . . ."

Samantha's voice dwindled as she realized that Jessica wasn't paying any attention to her at all. What she was looking at interested her much . . . much . . . more.

JESSICA'S EYES were locked on a boy across from them who was studying a model of the *Titanic* encased in glass. He was lanky, with longish sandy-blond hair, and dressed plainly in black pants and a denim work shirt. Even from across the gift shop, his sparkling blue eyes were striking.

Samantha had never seen such a good-looking boy. How old was he? She decided he couldn't be more than fifteen.

At first he was so engrossed in the *Titanic* model that he didn't notice the sisters staring at him. Then, as though he felt the touch of their eager glances, he lifted his head, turning his face in their direction.

What a brilliant smile he had! Samantha returned it, her eyes shining. There was a definite connection between them. She had never felt it with any boy before, but this electric thing that had zapped back and forth was all she'd ever imagined.

Glancing at her sister, Samantha saw that Jessica seemed to think he was smiling at *her*. Jessica tossed back her lustrous dark hair, lowered her lids, and quirked her mouth into a flirty half smile.

Samantha slid her eyes back to the boy, trying not to appear obvious. Which one of them was he smiling at? She'd been certain he was smiling at her, but now she wasn't as sure.

This time Samantha's phone rang. Once more, it was her mother. Samantha accepted the call without even saying hello. "We're leaving now, Mom. Promise."

Samantha turned to tell Jessica they had to go but Jessica was already hurrying across the shop, making a beeline for the same door by which the boy was departing. Was he also going to be on the *Titanic 2*?

If so, Samantha didn't want her sister talking to him. "Oh, no, you don't, Jess," Samantha mumbled as she quickly followed. "He smiled at me first."

• • •

"This is ours!?" Samantha squealed happily. "We have our *own* room!" The Burnett family stood in a small cabin marked 266. It had a round porthole window, two twin beds, and a wardrobe.

"We'll be right next door," their mother explained. "See, there's even an adjoining door."

"I love this cabin! It's so old-fashioned," Jessica said gleefully, throwing her suitcase on one of the twin beds.

"This ship is an exact replica of the original *Titanic*," their father said.

"I hope the rudder isn't the same," Samantha worried. She held up one of the pamphlets on the table. "This says they now think the ship sank because of a design flaw in the rudder."

"This ship is actually state-of-the-art," their mother said. "It only *looks* like the original. Believe me, I checked before we booked this trip."

A man in a crisp navy-blue uniform knocked on the open cabin door. "Mr. and Mrs. Burnett?" he inquired.

"That's us," Mr. Burnett replied.

"I'm Joe Rodgers, ship steward. I have some bad news and some great news."

"Well, maybe that's good," Mr. Burnett joked. "What is the bad news?"

"We accidentally double booked your room, two-sixty-five."

"You're right. That's bad," Mrs. Burnett said.

"But the great news is that we can upgrade you to a suite in first class."

Mr. and Mrs. Burnett's eyes lit excitedly. Then Mrs. Burnett frowned. "But we'll be so far from the girls."

"Oh, that's not a problem!" cried Jessica. Samantha knew what her sister was thinking. No "Lights out!" No "Keep it down in there!" No "This place is a mess!"

"We'll be fine," Samantha confirmed.

"See? They'll be okay," Mr. Burnett said to his wife. "And we're not that far away."

The smile returned to Mrs. Burnett's face. "Girls, you'll have to text me every hour," she told them.

"We will," the girls singsonged.

"I'll show you to your new room," Joe Rodgers offered. "Someone will come to pick up your bags shortly."

With a wave to their daughters, the Burnetts followed the steward out. When they were gone, Jessica did a quick, celebratory salsa step. "We won't see them again the rest of this trip. It'll be as if we're on our own."

Samantha had to admit that not having their parents watching their every move did make this cruise seem more exciting. She flopped backward onto her bed, while Jessica continued her happy dance.

Dreamily Samantha remembered the boy in the gift shop. He'd left the museum around the time the ship was boarding. Was he on this ship? How could she get away from Jessica for a while to try to find him?

Samantha noticed a scratching sound from behind the wall at the head of the two twin beds. "What's that?"

Jessica listened intently. *Scratch. Scratch-scratch. Scratch.* "I don't know."

Samantha put her ear to the wall to hear it better. Something was behind there, moving. It didn't scurry like a rodent, but she definitely heard movement and . . . breathing.

"Could it be Morse code?" Jessica wondered.

Samantha looked at her quizzically.

"It's a code of dots and dashes. People use it to communicate with either a telegraph machine or lights. Or tapping."

"You think someone behind the wall is sending us a secret message?" Samantha asked doubtfully.

"I don't know," Jessica admitted.

"I don't know, either. But it's kind of creepy."

In the open doorway stood a frowning, pale woman in a long green velvet dress, wearing an enormous feathered hat. "Dead or alive?" she inquired in a flat voice.

Samantha sat up on her bed as she gaped at the woman.

"What did you say?" Jessica asked.

"Dead or alive?"

"Uh, alive," Samantha answered. "We're alive."

"Don't be so sure," the woman said ominously.

THE PALE woman in the large hat and old-fashioned gown stepped into the room and glowered at them. "Who knows who will live and who will die?" she spoke with an eerie sing-song. She pointed her finger back and forth between Jessica and Samantha. "Maybe you will drown! Or you!"

Jessica held her cell phone up in front of her like someone in a movie using garlic or a cross to ward off a vampire. "I have my parents on speed dial," she warned. "If you come any closer, I'll press the button."

The woman tossed her head back, nearly unsettling her big hat, screaming with laughter. "I got you! I *so* got you! You should see your faces!"

"W-what?" Samantha stuttered.

"Our faces?" Jessica cried. "What happened to *your* face? You look like a ghost!"

"That's exactly what I'm supposed to be. A ghost!" The woman was laughing so hard tears streamed from her eyes. "I didn't know if the white makeup would be too much, but I guess it worked. You two fell for it hook, line and sinker. Hilarious!"

"Okay! Okay! You got us," Samantha admitted, starting to smile. It *was* pretty funny that they'd been so easy to scare. "Great costume."

The woman slowed her laughter, wiping tears from her eyes. "Thanks. I've been planning this all year, and you were the first ones I've tested it on. I'd say it was a success."

"Is this supposed to be a *haunted* cruise?" Samantha asked. She knew the cruise was going to re-create the experience of being on the *Titanic*, but she hadn't heard anything about it being a ghostship.

"Not really," the woman said, waving her hand dismissively. "Though some of the crew are dressed as passengers from the original *Titanic*, so, in a way, they're sort of ghostly."

"Are you supposed to be someone famous?" Jessica asked.

"I'm glad you asked. Yes! I'm Molly Brown. She was a wealthy woman who was traveling back home from Europe. Reportedly she was very brave in the lifeboat and insisted that the oarsman pick up more people from the water than he thought the lifeboat could hold. She saved their lives!"

"Is that your job, to dress up and be Molly Brown?" Samantha inquired.

"I wish it was, but I have other duties. I'm Ashley Holmes, one of your cruise directors. It's my job to think of fun things to keep the passengers amused, like a costume room you'll be able to visit. We'll get you all done up as if you were really on the *Titanic* back in nineteen twelve. You'll love it."

"Ooh . . . fun!" Jessica crooned with a shiver of excitement.

"Wait — what were you saying about alive or dead?" Samantha reminded the cruise director.

"I almost forgot!" Ashley Holmes opened the green velvet bag that hung on her wrist and dug out two slips of paper. She handed one to each girl.

A name was written on each slip. "Alice Littlefield," Samantha read. Looking over at Jessica's slip, she read: "Matilda Littlefield."

"They were passengers on the *Titanic*," Ashley Holmes told them. "Every passenger gets one. I picked those especially for you girls because they were twins, too."

"We're not twins," Samantha told her.

A puzzled expression appeared on Ashley Holmes's face. "Really? I saw copies of your passport pictures and just assumed . . ."

"You didn't read our birth dates," Samantha told her. "We're a year and a half apart."

"It doesn't matter. You two look enough alike to be twins."

"Well, we're not," Jessica insisted.

"So anyway, girls," the cruise director said more seriously. "Let me tell you what these slips are for. There's a number on each slip that corresponds to a real passenger on the original *Titanic* voyage. If your number is the same as the number of a dead passenger, then you're dead. If the person whose number you are holding lived, then you've survived the journey."

"When will we find out?" Jessica asked.

"Hold on to your slip until the end of the voyage. We'll let you know your fate — or your passenger's fate." The smile faded from the cruise director's face. "As you leave the *Titanic*, we will tell you if your person was saved or drowned."

"Weren't all the women and children saved?" Samantha asked, recalling what she'd read online about the famous disaster. The women and children were put on the lifeboats first. When it was time for the men to go, there weren't any lifeboats left for most of them.

"Not *all* the women and children were saved, especially not those in the bottom of the ship, in third class. Many of them went down with the ship. Some women in first and second class chose to stay behind with their husbands," Ashley Holmes told them. "Is there anything further I can do for you?"

"We heard some kind of scratching behind that wall. Do you have any idea what it could be?"

"Oh, sound travels all over this ship. The walls are paper-thin. You can hear everything. Don't pay any attention to it," the cruise director said with a smile. "And watch what you say because everyone can hear you as well."

4

SAMANTHA AND Jessica waved as Ashley Holmes left. "There's a woman who loves her work," Jessica commented with wry amusement.

Samantha laughed lightly. "No kidding."

The scratching returned to the room. "Listen, Jess! Hear that?"

Joining Samantha, Jessica pressed her ear to the wall to listen. Whatever was behind there began to pant heavily.

Then, suddenly, the sounds stopped completely.

"It's gone," Jessica observed.

"Isn't that odd?" Samantha said.

"Very odd," Jessica agreed. "Let's just hope it doesn't come back."

Samantha nodded. Maybe the sound would just go away.

She glanced down at the numbered paper in her hand. The idea was really sort of clever, she decided. Who would live and who would die? It reminded her of the saying: When your number's up, it's up. But in this case, there was an actual number attached to it.

"I wonder if we live or die," Jessica mused, almost as though reading Samantha's mind.

"Not we, *them*!" Samantha reminded her. "The Littlefields. We're not *really* going to die."

"I suppose," Jessica agreed. "Still . . . I feel like we *are* them now."

"Well, we're not," Samantha insisted. "We're not them, it's not nineteen twelve, and we're not going to maybe drown when the ship sinks — which it's not going to!" She didn't like this whole idea. There was nothing appealing about taking on the character of someone who might meet her doom in a freak accident in the middle of the Atlantic Ocean. Besides, it all happened more than a hundred years in the past. "What do you like about all this?" she asked her sister.

Jessica shrugged. "It's kind of cool to feel like I'm back in time and on this famous ship. We get to dress up."

"But we're on a ship where people died," Samantha protested.

"You're taking it too seriously," Jessica advised. "This isn't the real *Titanic*. No one really died here."

"I suppose."

"Anyway, I'm hungry," Jessica announced. "I'm going to go find something to eat."

Samantha stretched and yawned. "Mind if I don't come with you? I'm not hungry, and we got up so early. I'd rather take a nap."

Jessica smiled happily. "Oh, that's great!"

Samantha shot her a puzzled expression. "Great?"

"Of course! Isn't it great to be on this cruise where we can nap whenever we feel tired, without Mom and Dad nagging us to do something else?" Jessica said, already backing toward the door as if she couldn't wait to get away.

What was Jessica up to? Samantha had never known her to be so enthusiastic about napping before.

"What was that?" Jessica asked, bending her head down. "Oops! It's my stomach grumbling. I'd better go. Want anything?"

Samantha locked Jessica in a suspicious gaze as she shook her head. "Have fun," she murmured.

Instantly, Jessica was gone from the room.

Samantha lay down on the bed, letting her feet dangle over the side. What was going on with Jessica? What could she be —

Samantha leaped to her feet as she realized what her sister had in mind. There was no way she was really hungry. They'd eaten less than an hour before. She wanted to go off by herself to find the cute boy from the Haunted Museum!

"Jess, you little sneak," Samantha grumbled. It didn't matter that she'd intended on doing the exact same thing. Samantha was annoyed that Jessica had beaten her to it.

Once more, scratching sounds came from behind the wall. Samantha knelt on the bed, pressing her ear to the wall. The scratching stopped and was replaced with whimpering, like that of a hurt child.

Had someone left a child alone in the cabin next door? As much as she wanted to chase after Jessica and the boy, if a child was in trouble, she had to do something.

Alarmed, Samantha went out into the hall to check. There was no cabin next door — only a wall with an air vent near the floor. As she stepped outside, she noticed that the number on the cabin door read 299.

"Two ninety-nine?" she questioned quietly. She'd been sure they were in 266.

Before she could give this further thought, a high-pitched whine filled the air.

Where could it be coming from?

Kneeling, Samantha peered into the swirling scrollwork covering the vents near the floor, but could see nothing but darkness. "Hello?" she called softly. "Who's in there? Are you all right?"

There was no response, so she tried again. "Anyone in there?"

"Looking for something?"

Samantha gazed up at Joe Rodgers, the steward from earlier. "I heard a noise in there," she told him.

"Probably just the heat coming up from the boiler. These April nights still get chilly."

"No," she disagreed. "I heard scratching and a child crying."

"A child crying?" he echoed. He squatted beside the vent and put his ear to it. "I don't hear anything," Joe said as he straightened. "There's no way anyone could be in there. It's completely sealed."

"But I heard it in my cabin," Samantha insisted.

"What cabin is that?"

"Two-ninety-nine, right behind me."

"You mean two-sixty-six."

Samantha turned toward the door. "No, two-nine . . ." Her words trailed off as she saw that the numbers on her door did, in fact, say 266. She felt completely disoriented. Where was she? But the moment passed. She had just come out that door.

"I remember you from earlier," Joe Rodgers said. "That's your cabin and it's two-sixty-six."

Joe Rodgers went into the cabin, looking around. "Where did the sound come from?"

Samantha stood in the doorway and pointed. "Over there, from the wall behind the beds."

While Joe Rodgers listened, occasionally tapping the wall, Samantha investigated the numbers fastened to the door. They didn't wiggle or budge. What was going on?

"I'm sure it was only the pipes you heard," Joe Rodgers confirmed. "Sometimes the air gets in them and they whistle a little. It might sound like crying to someone with an active imagination."

"Okay. Thanks for checking," Samantha said as the ship steward left. Closing the door behind her, she sighed. Of course it sounded unbelievable, but still . . . she'd heard it. She was sure. Placing the side of her head to the wall once again, she listened.

Silence.

Whatever it had been, it had gone away. She stood listening for several minutes more just to be certain, but the scratching and whimpering didn't return.

5

SAMANTHA LEFT her cabin and followed the signs pointing toward the Promenade Deck. It struck her that for such a luxurious ship, the white halls were plain and unadorned with paintings or posters of any kind. Overall, the feeling was one of functional simplicity.

The Promenade Deck was on the same level as her cabin. When she pushed open the heavy door, a warm, wet ocean breeze whipped her hair. Deck chairs lined the inside walls away from the ocean side of the deck. Some of the reclining chairs were already filled by people snuggled under blankets, reading or chatting with one another. A field of blue sky dotted with high, billowy clouds dominated the scene, and seagulls screamed in the distance.

With her raised palm, Samantha shielded her eyes from the sun's glare.

"Oh my gosh!" she murmured as the people walking the deck came into clearer view. It was as though she'd gone back in time. Women dressed in lovely dresses, some ankle-length and others to the ground. Samantha loved their oversize hats trimmed with feathers, fake flowers, and ribbons. Many of them strolled the deck on the arms of men in top hats and old-fashioned suits, carrying walking canes.

Mesmerized by the sight, Samantha stepped

out onto the deck. Jessica had been right. This *Titanic* cruise was really awesome.

"Pretty amazing, isn't it?"

Samantha turned around toward the young male voice that had spoken to her, and her eyes went wide with delight.

There he was — the boy from the gift shop!

Up close he was even better-looking than she'd thought. He wore a blue denim shirt, black pants, and boots. The ocean breeze stirred his thick hair. Samantha noticed that his nose had an attractive slope, and she liked the slight upward tilt of his strong chin.

So adorable!

"Yeah, the ship is really beautiful," Samantha replied, gazing into his vivid blue eyes.

"I'm John," he said, reaching out to shake her hand.

"I'm Sam. Samantha."

"I like Samantha better. Sam sounds too boy-ish for a pretty girl like you."

A pretty girl like me! For a second, Samantha was too stunned to breathe. *A pretty girl like me!*

Samantha beamed at him. "So, are you a passenger on this cruise?"

"I work here," he replied.

"Doing what?"

John smiled, and his teeth reminded Samantha of perfect white pearls. "I do whatever they need me to do. I'm the jack-of-all-trades."

Samantha was about to ask him if those were his real clothes or if he was playing a role. It was hard to tell. But she didn't want to take the chance of sounding rude, so she said nothing.

Still, her mind raced, scrambling to think of *something* to say to keep the conversation going on. The last thing she wanted was for him to wander off.

"The clothing is really interesting, isn't it?" Samantha remarked, at last.

"There's a room where they have costumes for cruise guests to wear — did you want to go find something?" John suggested.

"I guess . . ." She didn't want to leave him, though. "Will you be here when I get back?"

"Definitely," he assured her.

"I'll be right back, then," Samantha said as she turned to leave. "Right back!"

"I'll be here." John flashed his beautiful smile.

Samantha hesitated, hating to leave now that she'd found the one person she'd been looking for. What if Jessica came across him while she was gone?

Samantha went back inside and descended the nearest staircase she found, blinded by thoughts of John's deep blue eyes. She'd have to find a great costume, one that made her look older and more sophisticated. Something that Jessica would choose. Her sister had good taste in clothing. Better than Samantha's. Before meeting John, Samantha had never cared much about clothing, preferring comfort. But now it was important to look as attractive as possible.

Samantha suddenly stopped. She had *no* idea where she was going!

The bottom level apparently wasn't marked as clearly as the second-class section had been. There wasn't even anyone around to ask where to find the costumes. They all seemed to be out on the upper decks. "Hello?" Samantha called. "Anyone here?"

Samantha hurried down corridors, rounded corners, retraced her steps, and went down other hallways — until she was even more confused.

All this wasted time! She should never have come down here. John would probably have given up waiting for her and she'd never see him again.

"Ugh." Samantha groaned at that thought just as she neared a staircase that led to an upper floor. She thought it looked familiar and decided she could find her way back to John from her cabin.

When she finally got back to her cabin it was marked 299.

What was going on?

Samantha checked the door to the right: 267. The door to the left was marked 265.

Someone was clearly playing a joke on them, but it wasn't funny anymore. Taking her phone from her pocket she took a picture of her door. There! That proved it. It said 299!

As she pulled out her key, Samantha noticed that the door was slightly ajar, though she was pretty sure she'd shut it before leaving. "Jess?" Samantha called softly, opening the door wider.

6

J ESSICA'S BACK was turned toward Samantha
as she searched through the cabin, combing through
each of the still-empty dresser drawers.

"Oh, good. You're here," Samantha said. If
Jessica was here, it meant she wasn't on the deck
with John. "I got so lost trying to find the costume
room, but maybe you can help me?"

Samantha stepped inside and saw that Jessica
was wearing a black maid's uniform with a white

apron and ruffled mop cap. Black stockings and ankle-high boots completed the outfit. Of all the costumes she could have selected, why would she decide to be a maid? It wasn't like Jessica to pick such an unfashionable costume.

"What are you looking for?" Samantha asked as she stepped farther into the cabin.

"The locket! I have to find it!"

Samantha froze. The voice she'd just heard was high and raspy. It wasn't her sister's voice.

The figure turned.

It definitely wasn't Jessica.

Gaping, Samantha stared at the girl she had mistaken for her sister. No more than fifteen, the girl was thin and pretty but with pale skin and deep shadows beneath her dark, burning eyes. Her lips were dry and her hands trembled ever so slightly. Her dark hair hung lifelessly at the sides of her gaunt face.

Samantha couldn't stop staring.

"The locket — you stole it from me."

"What?" Samantha asked. "I didn't steal a locket from anyone. I don't know what you mean." She didn't like being around this girl. Samantha hoped she would leave right away. "Honestly, there's no locket here."

"You're lying," the girl insisted. "I know you are. Give it back to me."

As the girl spoke, her face was changing before Samantha's eyes. It appeared to be contorting into a different shape, shifting into someone — something — else.

"What are you doing?" Samantha asked, her voice a quaking whisper. Although she wanted to look away, she was too amazed to even turn her head.

When the girl replied, her voice dropped to a low growl. "I'm not doing anything."

"But your face," Samantha said, backing away.

"What about my face?" the girl asked in a snarl.

Samantha grabbed the doorknob as she realized what the face was becoming.

A skull!

And then a face.

And then a skull again.

Terrified, Samantha tried to scream, but only managed a horrified croak. In front of her stood a skeleton with a maid's uniform hanging from its bony frame.

It reached out a bony hand.

Samantha cringed as the skeleton touched her shoulder, shutting her eyes tightly to block out the horrible skull face. *Open your eyes*, Samantha commanded herself as she cowered against the door. *You've fallen asleep. This is a dream. Wake yourself up! Wake up!*

When Samantha forced herself to sneak a peek, the girl was no longer a skeleton. Once more she was the pale-faced girl with the dark-ringed eyes. "Where is the locket?" the girl demanded.

Samantha forced herself to speak despite her terror. "I saw a locket in the Haunted Museum; that's the only locket I know of."

"Don't lie! You took it."

"I didn't take it! Honest!"

Suddenly she realized what was going on. This was part of the cruise. A gimmick. A trick. It had to be.

"Wow! You really had me fooled," Samantha admitted as she searched in her canvas bag for some gum or a mint to moisten her dry mouth. Her hands were shaking, but she tried to keep her voice calm. "That is some amazing special effect, though."

The girl stood staring, saying nothing. Then, once more, she transformed into a skeleton.

Samantha's heart began to race again as the creature reached out for her. Its bony hand locked around her wrist. That was no special effect!

Samantha pulled away, but the skeleton held firm.

With another hard pull, Samantha broke free and fled. But where was she going? Once more lost in the maze of hallways, she finally came upon the sign pointing toward the Promenade Deck. Breathlessly she raced toward it.

7

T**HE** **SUN** blinded Samantha the moment she stepped outside. She drew in a deep breath and waited for her hammering heart to calm itself. What had happened was *not* her imagination. She noticed a red mark on her wrist where that *thing* had grabbed her.

Advancing out onto the deck, she searched among the costumed passengers, trying to locate John. From across the deck, a girl in a plumed hat with an enormous brim turned and stared at her — Jessica! She had on a short gold jacket and a narrow ankle-length skirt above low boots. At first Samantha was so interested in her sister's outfit that she didn't notice who she was with. But then, looking over her sister's shoulder, she saw that Jessica was talking to John!

Jessica turned back around and resumed the lively conversation she was having with the boy without acknowledging that she'd even seen her sister.

A mix of emotion washed over Samantha and she froze, paralyzed with indecision. Part of her was annoyed that Jessica had swooped in while she was gone and was now hogging John's attention. But another part of her was relieved to see her sister. The strange encounter with the skeleton maid had really scared her, and her sister was the one she wanted to tell about it.

Was she angry at Jessica, or was she incredibly thankful that she'd found her?

Samantha's path was blocked by a woman in a long gown with her hair swept into a bun — her mother. And following after her was Samantha's father, also dressed for the time period in a dark suit and round bowler hat.

"There you are!" Mrs. Burnett cried. "I've been texting and texting! Why haven't you answered me?"

Samantha pulled out her phone to check it, then held it under her mother's chin. "There are no bars, Mom!"

Mrs. Burnett took her own cell phone out of a small velvet bag that hung on her wrist and scowled down at it. She sighed, seeming perplexed.

Samantha took it from her and pointed to the screen. "See, Mom? *Sending failed*. It says it five times," Samantha pointed out impatiently.

"Oh, you're right," Mrs. Burnett admitted. "I didn't notice."

"Isn't that strange," Mr. Burnett remarked. "I'll have to inquire if there's Wi-Fi anywhere on the ship. They must have a business center."

"Maybe they've blocked cell phones to keep up the atmosphere of the *Titanic*. All these beautiful costumes would look very odd if everyone had cell phones, laptops, and tablets going," Mrs. Burnett considered.

"I guess you're right," Mr. Burnett said with a chuckle.

Stepping back, Mrs. Burnett studied Samantha critically. "Why aren't you in costume? You look so out of place," she remarked.

"Mom! Dad! Something really scary just happened. A horrible creature is snooping around in my and Jessica's cabin."

"A horrible creature?" Mr. Burnett asked.

"I'm not sure. A skeleton! A ghost! She grabbed me. Look!" Samantha held up her bruised wrist.

"She?" Mr. Burnett inquired.

"The thing was dressed as a maid. It looked like a girl a little older than me. But then its face changed into a skull."

"There are all kinds of actors and special effects on this cruise," Mrs. Burnett said doubtfully. "You can't let it scare you."

"Mom, it *was* real. Besides that, there's a strange scratching, crying sound behind our wall."

"It's probably just the heat coming up," Mr. Burnett said.

"And the number of our cabin keeps changing."

"Now you're just being ridiculous," Mrs. Burnett scoffed. "How could that be possible? You're in cabin two-sixty-six."

"Only sometimes!" Samantha said. "Sometimes

we're in cabin two-sixty-six, and other times it changes to two-ninety-nine."

"That's impossible," Mrs. Burnett insisted.

"I can prove it!" Samantha cried. "This ship doesn't have bars but my phone camera still works." At least she hoped it did. "I took a picture."

With her fingers moving quickly, Samantha accessed the photos on her phone. "Here! I've got it. Wait until you see this!"

Samantha found the picture she'd taken of her cabin door. "There!" she cried as she held the screen up for her parents to see.

"I can't make out the numbers on the door," Mr. Burnett said.

Samantha hit zoom and the photo came into focus.

"Two-sixty-six," Mr. Burnett read.

"No way!" Samantha snapped the phone back and peered at it. 266! This couldn't be happening.

When she'd taken the shot it had said 299. She was positive! *Positive!*

"Maybe you still have jet lag," Mrs. Burnett suggested. "We arrived in England only yesterday after all."

"Mom! It's not jet lag!" Samantha wailed. Why wouldn't they believe her?

"Why don't you go get a costume, sweetie," Mrs. Burnett advised. "It will put you into the spirit of things."

"Don't say the word *spirit*," Samantha grumbled. "I'm starting to think there are spirits on this ship — evil spirits!"

"Samantha, don't get carried away," her father warned. "Maybe you should take a nap."

"I have to talk to Jessica first."

"Where is she?" Mr. Burnett asked.

"Right behind you, over there," Samantha said, pointing. She peered between her parents as they turned, looking for Jessica, but she wasn't there. Neither was John.

Samantha sighed in frustration. Her sister had moved on while Samantha was talking to their parents. "Never mind. I'll go get a costume," Samantha agreed, annoyed that they had kept her from getting to John and Jessica and that they wouldn't believe her. She took a few steps, then hesitated. She didn't want to go back to the bottom of the ship again — especially not by herself.

"Would you walk me there?" she requested, suddenly uneasy about going back inside the ship. "I'm scared."

"Oh, all right," her mother agreed, "but you're being silly."

"I'm not being silly," Samantha insisted. She was absolutely sure that all this wasn't her imagination. But was she losing her mind? *That*, she decided, was a definite possibility.

SAMANTHA AND her parents reached a door down in third class where a sign was posted, reading: WARDROBE DEPARTMENT: PASSENGERS WELCOME.

"Here it is," Mr. Burnett said.

"Pick something nice, dear. We'll see you for supper," Mrs. Burnett added as she turned to go.

"Don't leave me!" Samantha implored.

"Come on now," Mr. Burnett said with a smile.

"There's nothing to be afraid of. Where's that independent Samantha we know and love?"

She wishes she was home hiding under her covers, Samantha thought uneasily.

A plaque on the door read: ASHLEY HOLMES. It made Samantha feel a little braver; at least she'd met the woman before.

"Okay, see you later," Samantha said to her departing parents. When Samantha went into the room, Ashley Holmes sat at a small desk, no longer dressed as Molly Brown. Blond curls bounced around her heart-shaped face as she looked up from the magazine she was reading to greet Samantha.

"Hi, again. Did something happen to your costume?"

"You must be thinking of my older sister. She was in here earlier. Remember? We're not really twins but we look a lot alike."

Ashley Holmes once more threw her head back

with laughter. "Oh, that's right! Of course! Silly me!" She rose from her desk. "Nice to meet you again. They have me doing everything around here. Just everything!"

Samantha remembered that John had made a similar remark about himself. "I guess that's how they run things."

"It sure is," Ashley Holmes agreed. She made circles in the air with her fingers. "It never stops! It's always go-go-go! This evening at dinner I'll be singing with the musicians who are acting the part of the string quartet that played as the ship sank."

"Wow!" Samantha gasped. "That was brave."

"I know!" Ashley Holmes agreed, shaking her head. She leaned in closer, dropping her voice to a confidential tone. "They didn't really have a girl singer, but we take small liberties with the truth here and there. After dinner I'll be giving fox-trot lessons."

"Fox-trot?" Samantha questioned.

"It was a popular dance at the time."

"Sounds fun."

"Let's hope so! Well, what would you like to be — an aristocrat, a servant, an immigrant?" Ashley Holmes asked.

"What was Jess?" Her sister looked great in her costume. Whatever she'd picked, that's what Samantha wanted to be.

"She was an aristocrat: first class all the way."

"Then that's what I want to be, please," Samantha requested.

Ashley started by pulling Samantha's hair into an elegant updo, using a curling iron to form loose spiral curls to frame her face. "Finishing touch," the woman remarked, attaching a fluffy, pink plume to the side of Samantha's hair.

Then she pulled several items from the racks of clothing that filled the huge space. She handed

them to Samantha and indicated a row of changing rooms.

When Samantha had changed into her outfit,
she studied herself in the full-length mirror behind
the door. "I love it," she said softly. Ashley had
selected a maroon dress that fell in a straight line
from her armpits to her ankles; tiny gold beads
were sewn in vertical lines to make delicate golden
stripes. On her feet she wore velvet t-strap pumps.

"Since you're young, I wanted to give you a
more modern look," Ashley Holmes explained.
"By nineteen-twelve, the straight lines of the flap-
per era were already starting to appear in ladies'
fashion, especially for the more daring."

"Wow," Samantha said, turning to admire the
feather in her hair and the delicate beading on
the back collar of the dress. "It's perfect."

"You look wonderful," Ashley Holmes confirmed.

"Thank you," Samantha said with a smile. It felt good to smile. She hadn't smiled in hours, not since seeing John. Thinking of John made her check her image in the mirror once more. She did look pretty, and Samantha couldn't wait for him to see her.

Thanking the woman with a curtsy (she couldn't help herself in the old-fashioned clothes), Samantha left. Her mother had been right. Getting into costume did make her feel more in the swing of things. It was almost as if she had been transported back to the *Titanic* of 1912.

This time, she made it to the second level without losing her way. As she neared her cabin, she saw Jessica coming toward her from the other end of the hall.

"Where have you been?" Samantha demanded.

But as angry as she felt toward her sister, Samantha was also glad to see her. Jessica was her older sister and her closest friend, and Samantha wanted to tell her everything that had happened.

Jessica smiled. "I have so much to tell you, Sam," she gushed.

"Jess, wait," Samantha ordered. "What number is our cabin?"

Jessica checked the numbers on the door. "Two sixty-six!"

"Sometimes when I look at it, the number is two-sixty-six, and at other times it says two-ninety-nine. I'm not imagining it."

"That's odd," Jessica said.

"*Odd* is not the word!" Samantha cried. "It's completely freaky!"

Jessica shrugged and unlocked the cabin door. "It's probably just Ashley Holmes and one of her bizarre gags," she decided, unconcerned, as they entered the cabin. "So, anyway, listen . . . this is what I want to tell you." She plunked down on her bed and faced Samantha. "Did you notice a really cute guy in the Haunted Museum gift shop?"

Samantha nodded. "Yeah." Instantly she felt bad about being annoyed with Jessica. Her sister hadn't even realized that she was interested in John.

"Well, he's on this ship and I talked to him. He's so nice!"

"I talked to him, too."

Jessica raised her eyebrows, surprised. "You did?"

"Yes. He's really nice. You're right."

"So nice," Jessica agreed. "And guess what? I think he likes me," she reported gleefully.

I was pretty sure he liked me, Samantha thought gloomily.

"Hey, I love your outfit," Jessica said, seeming to notice it for the first time. "Mine's so old-fashioned."

"Yours is pretty, too. The hat is great."

"Want to trade?" Jessica asked.

Samantha was tempted. It would be fun to wear the huge hat. But she liked her own outfit even better. "Maybe later," she allowed.

Shrugging, Jessica pulled out the long pin stuck in her upswept hair that held the hat in place. "Okay, later. Don't forget."

"Jess, do you believe in ghosts?" Samantha asked.

"I don't know," Jessica admitted. "I suppose anything is possible. Why?"

Her parents had called her silly. Would Jessica also dismiss her story?

"Something really strange happened before," Samantha told her sister.

SAMANTHA STUDIED her sister as Jessica listened to the story of the strange maid rummaging through their things. She seemed to be taking Samantha seriously. "I'm not crazy, Jess. She was so creepy," Samantha concluded.

"What did you say she was searching for?" Jessica asked.

"A locket."

Jessica reached into the space between her mattress and the box spring and withdrew something. "Like this?" she asked in a serious tone.

Samantha gaped in disbelief at the silver locket that lay in Jessica's outstretched palm. A lily was etched on the top of it. Samantha knew exactly where she'd seen it before. "Jessica," she said quietly. "Please tell me you didn't steal that from the Haunted Museum."

"I didn't."

Samantha had never known Jessica to shoplift or to lie — at least not about important things, and not to Samantha. But here was the evidence right in the palm of her sister's hand. "You could've gotten caught. Arrested! Are you crazy?!"

"I didn't steal it! Sam, you've got to believe me. I found it in my bag when I was looking for some lip balm before. I don't know how it got there."

"If you didn't steal it, then why did you hide it?" Samantha challenged. Her sister's story just didn't make sense.

"I just stuck it under here because I didn't know what else to do with it. I knew you wouldn't believe me. I couldn't believe it, either. I swear! I don't know how it got into my bag."

"Well, whatever that creature was who was tearing this cabin apart — it wants the locket back," Samantha informed Jessica.

"Do you really think this is what it wanted?" Jessica asked.

"I'd say there's an excellent chance of that. Yes!" Samantha sat beside Jessica on the bed. "What are we going to do?" she asked.

"Give it back," Jessica replied.

"To the Haunted Museum or to that creature?" The idea that she would have to see that horrifying girl once more was awful enough. Would she actually have to reach out to give her the locket? And when she did, would she touch the ghostly palm or — even worse — the bones of a skeletal hand?

"Why do you suppose it wants this locket so badly?" Jessica wondered. Sliding her fingernail along the side of the locket, Jessica popped it open. "Hah!" she laughed lightly in surprise.

"What?" Samantha demanded, sliding closer to her sister. The old photos in the locket were as blurred and ruined as when they'd seen them in the Haunted Museum.

"So that doesn't tell us anything," Jessica said.

"No," Samantha agreed.

"You're not kidding me, are you? You really did see a ghost or something that wanted this locket?" Jessica checked.

"I really saw it, Jess. It nearly scared me to death. I don't ever want to see it again."

"But why would she even want the locket?"

"Who knows?!" Samantha cried. "Who knows why it jumped into your bag and followed you onto the ship?"

"I'm telling you the truth," Jessica said. "I did not steal it."

In her heart Samantha believed her sister. It wasn't any more bizarre than everything else that had happened that day.

"Why are these things happening to us?" Jessica asked. "Haunted lockets are following me, and you're seeing skeletons."

"I don't know." Did Samantha even believe in ghosts? Before today she would have said she absolutely did not. Now she wasn't so sure.

Jessica returned the locket to its hiding place. "I don't think we should tell anyone about having the locket," she said. "No one will believe I didn't steal it. When we get home, I'll mail it back to the Haunted Museum."

"Okay," Samantha agreed. "I won't say anything."

Jessica unlaced her boots and wiggled out of her narrow skirt. "I'll tell you one thing, these clothes are not comfortable," she commented. "Ashley Holmes told me this is called a hobble skirt."

"Hobble?" Samantha asked.

"As in 'to cripple.' The skirt is so narrow you can't walk normally in it. You have to take tiny little steps."

"I guess they thought that was ladylike," Samantha suggested.

After changing into a T-shirt and soft, checked flannel pants, Jessica inhaled deeply. "That's better. I can breathe again." She flopped on her bed and listened to her iPod. Soon her eyes were closed and she was nodding her head to the beat playing in her ears.

How could she be so calm? Jessica always had a way of putting her worries aside. Samantha wished she could be more like that.

Samantha changed into sweats, careful to hang up her costume and put her plumed headpiece safely on top of the dresser. She rummaged for the magazine in her canvas bag and stretched out onto her bed to peruse it. But she'd been up early and it had been a long, busy day. Soon she laid her head on the pillow, drifting into a dreamless sleep.

• • •

When Samantha awoke, the room was awash in a gray-blue dusk coming from the porthole window. How long had she slept? According to the digital readout on her cell phone, she'd been out for nearly two hours! It was suppertime.

Rolling over, she saw that Jessica wasn't in her bed. If Jessica had wanted to go out, why hadn't she woken her up?

"I know why," Samantha muttered as she crossed to the wardrobe for her costume. She was probably looking for more *alone* time with John.

Opening the wardrobe door, Samantha cried out. Jessica's costume was still hung up, but Samantha's maroon frock was gone — and so was the feather headpiece. "Jessica!" Samantha growled.

The big hat that went with Jessica's outfit no longer intrigued Samantha. She wanted an elegant dress like the one she'd had — the one Jessica had taken.

There were more dresses in the wardrobe department. She'd hurry down to get another, a better one. She'd wear it to dinner and look unbelievable in it. That would catch John's attention.

Samantha hoped she remembered the way down to the wardrobe department on C Deck. The hallways of the ship were such a maze of identical corridors. She was relieved when she came to a curved stairway with an arrow pointing down and marked: THIRD CLASS — STEERAGE.

Before going down, she hesitated as gooseflesh sprung up on her arms. It was more than a passing chill. The cold seemed to seep all the way into her bones. Coupled with that was the distinct feeling that she wasn't alone.

Gazing around the hallway, Samantha saw no one, not even a shadow. But, just the same, she couldn't shake the eerie sensation. "Who's there?" she whispered.

No one responded, and so Samantha continued on, stepping down into the winding staircase — desperately hoping that whatever it was that she'd sensed wouldn't follow her down.

10

In a few minutes, Samantha was outside the wardrobe department. Turning the door handle, she discovered it was locked. "Hello?" she called as she rapped on the door, her voice sounding loud in the silent hall. "Hello, Ms. Holmes?"

Samantha called out several more times, hoping that Ashley Holmes might still be nearby. After a few more minutes, she ambled away from the wardrobe department, gazing around the empty hallway. The halls were narrower here and the ceilings lower. Clearly this was the plain, no-frills part of the ocean liner. Samantha remembered reading that the people who stayed down here were poor folks looking for an inexpensive way to get to America. The servants slept down here also, as well as the men who worked in the boiler rooms.

Samantha shuddered as that same cold blast from before blew by. Once more, gooseflesh crept across her skin and she felt as though icy fingers were touching her bare arms.

"Go away!" she shouted, feeling foolish and yet somehow sure some invisible presence was nearby.

Moving down the hall, Samantha came to a cabin whose door was slightly ajar. Maybe some-one in there could tell her if the wardrobe room was closed. Or how to get back up to the dining room. In truth, all she really cared about was not being alone anymore.

Cautiously Samantha peered in. The room was small, with a bunk bed across from a single bed. The only other furniture was a coatrack and a plain desk. The walls were plain, as were the curtains and bed linens. It was far different from the nice room she and Jessica shared. There wasn't a bit of luxury here.

Samantha jumped with surprise as her cell phone suddenly rang.

Grabbing for the phone in her pocket, she checked the screen. Still no service! *Private Caller* was the only identification. "Hello?" Samantha asked in a puzzled, wary tone.

All she heard on the other end was the howl of a hard-blowing wind. At least that was what it sounded like to Samantha.

"Hello?" she asked again, her voice rising. "Who's there?"

"Alice Littlefield?" the low, croaking voice on the other end asked. "Is that you, Alice?"

Samantha froze. She knew that voice. It was the ghost skeleton from earlier. "My name's not Alice . . . whoever," Samantha protested in a quavering voice. "You have the wrong person."

"Alice Littlefield," the voice repeated. "I know it's you. Stay away from him."

"Who?"

"You know who. He's mine."

Samantha breathed deeply to steady her nerves and was irritated that when she next spoke her voice still quivered with fear. "I don't know who you mean. Is this a joke?"

A high, enraged shriek poured from the phone. It was so shrill that Samantha threw her phone and clamped her hands over her ears. But it kept coming, filling the hallway until Samantha was down on her knees, wincing from the pain that was searing her brain, making everything a red blur.

Samantha felt she couldn't stand it another moment, that she would shatter into pieces.

Abruptly the deafening scream stopped.

It was replaced by total silence.

Slowly Samantha lifted her head and listened to the quiet. She couldn't hear the hum of the ship's engines or the crash of the waves.

Had she gone deaf? Did the nightmarish scream blow out her eardrums?

Samantha tapped the wall with her fingernails to check. The *click click* sound was there. That was a relief. Just the same, the hallway was eerily silent. Too silent.

Uneasy, Samantha darted toward the stairway she'd come down. When she finally reached it, Samantha was dismayed to discover that a black iron gate had been drawn across the doorway.

"What next?" Samantha grumbled as she realized that the gate wouldn't give way when she pushed it. Rattling the bars, she shouted up the stairway. "Hey! Anybody up there? I'm stuck down here. Anybody?"

From somewhere nearby, a baby started to wail. It was coming from one of the cabins. Samantha went toward the sound, knocking on the door. "Hello?"

The crying grew louder. Samantha pressed her ear to the door. Inside, people were murmuring in urgent whispers. There were a lot of voices, all talking at once; too many, it seemed, to all be in such a small cabin.

They would never hear her knocking, so she pulled the door open.

The room appeared empty. Yet Samantha was bombarded with panicked voices all speaking at once, their frantic words overlapping.

"They've locked us in."

"Let us out!"

"We'll drown down here."

The baby kept up its crying.

Was it a recording of some kind?

Samantha stepped into the room and immediately her heart began to pound. So much emotion! Anger. Terror. Desperation. Sweat formed on her forehead. She clutched at her throat as she felt it grow dry.

"We're all going to die!" a woman shouted. Samantha whirled toward the voice that came from behind her, but no one was there.

What was going on? It was horrible! She had to get out of there.

Samantha raced out of the narrow, terror-filled cabin and back to the gate, shaking it with all her strength. "Let me out! Somebody open this gate! Open it! Please!"

Then she heard something move on the other side. Had someone heard her?

As Samantha looked up expectantly, she saw what was coming. Not a person but a torrent of surging water.

Pivoting on her heels, she raced down the hall, hoping to escape the powerful wave. There had to be another way out — had to be!

The foaming swirl of icy cold rushed down with such tremendous power that it knocked Samantha forward off her feet. She flailed helplessly, tossed beneath the freezing ocean waters.

Pushing upward, her arms were pinned by the force of the flood. Without thinking clearly, she tried to call for help and saw a stream of air bubbles cascade from her lips.

The last sound Samantha heard before passing out was that of a dog barking.

11

"SAMANTHA? SAMANTHA!"

Slowly Samantha opened her eyes. Jessica was staring down at her with a worried expression. "I've been looking all over for you. What happened?" Jessica asked. She knelt beside Samantha, still wearing the maroon beaded dress she'd "borrowed" from her little sister.

Sitting up, Samantha gazed at her surroundings, remembering everything that had happened.

But where was all the ocean water? There wasn't even a puddle anywhere.

"How did you get down here?" she asked her sister.

"What do you mean? I just walked down to look for you," Jessica replied. Samantha glanced across the hallway at the iron gate and saw it had been opened.

"I found you lying on the floor here. Are you all right?" Jessica asked.

Samantha opened her mouth to speak, but no words came out. How could she explain this?

"Why are your clothes wet? What happened?" Jessica pressed.

Clutching at her sweatshirt, Samantha realized it was soaked. So was her hair.

"My hair's wet!" she cried, filled with relief. It proved that what she had just experienced hadn't been her imagination or even a dream. Samantha grabbed Jessica by the wrist. "You're not going to believe what happened to me. But it really happened."

"What? Tell me!"

"I heard voices down here. People were crying because they were trapped and the ship was sinking. It was so scary. And then the ocean started pouring in and I went under." Tears of fear suddenly leaped to her eyes as she recalled it all. "I was sure I was going to drown."

Until Jessica wrapped her in a hug, Samantha hadn't realized she was trembling. Now all the terror of facing certain doom came over her and she shook even harder. "I was so sure I was going to die," she gasped breathlessly. "Jess, this ship! I think it's haunted. It has to be. I'm not crazy. I'm not making this up."

"I believe you," Jessica said.

"You do?" Samantha checked hopefully.

"Yeah. Look at what happened to me with the locket. You saw me put it under the mattress, didn't you?"

Samantha nodded.

"Well, when I went to dinner, I left it there in our cabin. But when I met Mom and Dad outside the restaurant, I looked down and — I was wearing it!"

Samantha stared at Jessica, shocked. "What did you do?"

"I screamed," Jessica reported. "I made a total scene. Mom and Dad looked like they wanted to disappear. Everyone thought I was crazy. And that cute John guy was in the room. He saw the whole thing. I could just die from embarrassment!"

Samantha felt too shaken-up to take any pleasure from her sister's humiliation in front of John. Instead she was simply glad not to be experiencing these things alone.

"I hid that locket in our wardrobe and locked it," Jessica added. "I know I didn't put it on, Sam. I'm sure of it."

"I believe you," Samantha said as she checked her phone. There was water behind the screen. "Do you have cell service?" she asked.

"No. Nobody does. They're trying to re-create the atmosphere of the original *Titanic*."

"I didn't, either." Samantha recalled the chilling call before she'd nearly drowned. "But the maid spoke to me over the phone. I recognized her voice. One minute it's all wispy, the next she's like a beast, growling and snarling her words. She shrieked so loudly into the phone I felt like I was about to shatter."

"When the voice spoke to you, before it started screaming, what did it say?" Jessica asked.

"It was telling me to stay away from some guy."

"Who?"

Shaking her head, Samantha shrugged. Jessica stood and drew Samantha to her feet. "You're shaking. You should get out of those wet clothes," she advised.

Samantha realized that, in addition to trembling, her teeth were also chattering. "You're right. I'm freezing," she admitted as they began to walk up the stairway to B Deck.

"Why were you even down there at all, Sam?"

As they stepped out onto the deck, Samantha wrapped her arms around herself for protection from the wet chilled air. "Because *someone* took my dress!" she replied accusingly, suddenly reminded that she was annoyed with Jessica.

Jessica smiled sheepishly. "We talked about switching, and I didn't want to wake you."

"Since when?" Samantha challenged. Jessica had never been overly concerned about disturbing

Samantha's sleep before. "You just wanted to take the dress without discussing it anymore."

"You could have worn my costume," Jessica countered.

"I'm not going to squeeze into that narrow hobble skirt and take teeny, tiny steps."

"That's why I didn't want it, either."

"Then you should have returned it."

Just then a tall man walked by. He was dressed in a casual white jacket and loose-fitting pants that flapped in the evening breeze. He wore a flat-topped, brimmed boater hat and smoked a pipe. With him was a pretty woman who was much younger than he was. Her frothy crepe dress fluttered about her, and she pulled her shawl more closely around her slender shoulders. Her lovely face was bathed in worry, and she clasped his arm.

"Why does he look so familiar?" Samantha asked Jessica. "I feel like we know him from somewhere."

"We do!" Jessica replied excitedly. "We saw him at the Haunted Museum. He's John Jacob Astor. Remember? The billionaire who saved the dogs? He was one of the mannequins in the glass cases. The woman with him must be his wife. I read that they were coming home from their honeymoon in Europe."

Samantha noticed that they both seemed distressed. "Kitty!" the man called, looking around. "Kitty, where are you, girl?"

"Oh, they've lost their cat," Jessica sympathized.

"Oh my gosh!" Samantha cried, suddenly realizing what she was seeing. "They're not searching for a cat, Jess. They've lost their dog."

"Oh, yeah. I remember," Jessica recalled. "I hope they find her."

"Maybe we can help," Samantha suggested. She turned to where she'd last seen Astor and his wife, but they weren't there. It was as if they'd disappeared. "Strange," Samantha muttered, ruffling the top of her hair.

"Oh well," Jessica said. "They'll find her. There's really nowhere she can go here on a ship. She's bound to turn up."

"I guess so," Samantha agreed. She stopped as a disturbing idea seized her. "Those were actors playing the part of the Astors, right?"

"Of course," Jessica confirmed, but seeming nervous just the same. "They're doing a terrific job with the makeup and costumes, aren't they?"

"That guy looked almost *exactly* like the mannequin we saw in the Haunted Museum," Samantha reminded her sister.

"No, no, they were actors," Jessica insisted, hurrying them along.

They headed directly to their cabin on the second level. "I wonder what the door number will be when we get there this time," Samantha said, fishing for the room key she'd stuck in her pocket.

"Yeah, I wonder, too," Jessica agreed distractedly as she looked at the screen of her cell phone. She waved it slowly in the air and Samantha knew her sister was hoping to find any hidden cell service.

When they were in front of the door, Samantha was happy to see that the numbers there were 266. "Hey, Jess! Good news! The door says two-sixty-six. At least that's normal, anyway," she reported, turning back toward her sister. "Maybe everything will . . ."

Samantha's words fell away as she looked at Jessica.

"What?" Jessica questioned, noticing Samantha's stricken expression. "Sam, what is it?"

Samantha's throat had dried up completely. She couldn't find the words to tell Jessica what she was seeing, so she pointed at her sister's collarbone.

"I don't believe it," Jessica breathed.

She was wearing the silver locket!

"Get it off me!" Jessica shouted, clutching at her throat. "Sam, I'm not kidding! I want it off me!"

Samantha leaped behind Jessica and tried to work open the locket's clasp. "Stop moving!" she demanded. "I can't get it with you jumping around like that."

Jessica forced herself to stand still. "Take it off! Take if off!" she whimpered impatiently.

Finally Samantha flicked the latch, and the locket fell to the floor. Instantly Jessica kicked it down the hall. Running to meet it, she kicked it again, even farther away. "There!" she announced triumphantly. "Now that ghost maid can pick it up, and she's welcome to it."

"I hope so," Samantha agreed. Maybe getting rid of the locket was all it would take to make their troubles go away. She really hoped so.

THE FOLLOWING morning after breakfast, Samantha and Jessica entered a luxurious room of brocade couches, polished wooden furniture, and glistening crystal chandeliers. Elaborate flower arrangements of hydrangeas and magnolias adorned the tables, and richly colored glass Tiffany shades shimmered above their silver lamp stands. It was a replica of the *Titanic*'s first-class reading and writing lounge. Shelves of leather-bound books lined the walls.

The girls hadn't bothered to wear their costumes, since Samantha had been terrified of venturing back down to the wardrobe room. Now, in her jeans, cotton hoodie, and flip-flops, Samantha felt completely out of place in this elaborate and ornate ballroom.

According to the cruise brochure, within the reading and writing lounge there was a lounge open to the first-class passengers only, with a special exhibit telling all about the history of the original *Titanic*. Although Samantha and Jessica weren't technically first-class passengers, their parents were, and it seemed like a good destination for gathering information that might shed some light on exactly what was going on.

Jessica headed for a dark wooden wall covered with faded photos, yellowed news clippings, and drawings. "These weren't in this room originally, though," she asked. "Were they?"

"How could they have been?" Samantha replied. "Some of these articles are about the day it sank."

"Then this part of the ship isn't an exact re-creation," Jessica said.

"No, I guess not," Samantha agreed. "The wardrobe room can't be the exact same either. So the ship isn't one hundred percent the same then."

"I sure hope they have more lifeboats," Jessica added.

"They must have," Samantha said, but she felt a little shiver of worry, just the same.

Together, they perused the wall of framed artifacts. While Jessica became engrossed in a news article about the launching of the "unsinkable" *Titanic*, Samantha went down the row of portraits of the passengers, crew, and employees.

Samantha stopped short at one old photo,

riveted by the faces in front of her. It showed the serving staff of the ship standing stiffly at attention, all dressed in their butler uniforms and maid outfits.

With her nose nearly to the glass, Samantha studied each face until she found the one she was looking for. When she found it, her breath caught in her throat for a moment. She stared even closer.

"Jess! It's her," she said excitedly. "I've found her. She's in this photo."

Jessica was instantly beside her. "Who have you found?"

"The maid — the ghost!"

"The ghost?"

"The one who was in our cabin searching for the locket," Samantha insisted, certain she was right. The girl was exactly as she remembered her but without the pale, ghostly appearance. This girl was lively and young.

"Is there a list of names anywhere?" Jessica asked. They searched the area but all they found was a caption beside the photo that identified it as MAIDS AND BUTLERS OF THE *TITANIC*.

"I wonder if we can find out anything about her," Samantha said. "There must be a list of servants somewhere."

"I wish our phones were working," Jessica added with a sigh. "We could search on the Internet."

"Our phones should work even without Wi-Fi. How are they doing this?" Samantha said, frustrated to be so cut off from the rest of the world.

"I don't know," Jessica admitted.

At a center table was a model of the ship, much like the one John had been interested in back at the Haunted Museum gift shop, only larger. It was encased in glass. Jessica and Samantha gazed at it, fascinated at every tiny detail. Even the passengers and crew were shown as miniaturized figures on the decks. Samantha knelt so that she was at eye level with the top A and B Decks of the model ship. "It's so detailed," she observed as her eyes traveled over the exquisitely intricate replication of every single element of the original ship.

Jessica came beside her, also kneeling. "Look at that," she said, pointing to one of the small model figures that populated the decks. "There's Astor, his wife, and the cute dog."

"And I see a figure of Molly Brown. She's wearing the same outfit Ashley Holmes wore yesterday morning," Jessica noticed. "See her sitting in a lounge chair?"

Samantha gripped Jessica's shoulder. "It's us. Right there! Look." Figures of two dark-haired girls stood next to the outer railing of the ship. One wore a big hat with a gold jacket and a hobble skirt, and the other had on a straight maroon dress and a feather in her upswept hair.

Jessica tapped the glass. "And that boy not far from them . . . doesn't he look sort of like John?"

Samantha had to admit that with its light hair, loose denim shirt, and straight pants, the figure did resemble John.

"Oh no," Samantha murmured.

"What is it?" Jessica asked.

Samantha tapped the glass, pointing to another of the miniature figures. It was a slim girl dressed in a maid's uniform. Her direction made it clear that she was walking directly toward the girls by the ship's railing. She carried a bundle in her hands, covered in white cloth. What was in it? A weapon of some kind?

"Let's get out of here," Samantha suggested, standing. "This room is giving me the creeps."

13

JESSICA LED them to a café, also in first class. "Dad showed me this place earlier. You've got to be starving."

"I am," Samantha admitted. Samantha and Jessica were the only customers in the café, and Samantha was glad that the place was casual, with wicker furniture and tropical, potted plants. A waiter in his twenties came to their

table and smiled. "I'm Trevor, and I'll be your
server tonight," he said.

"Is that how waiters spoke in nineteen-twelve?"
Jessica teased.

Trevor laughed as he handed them each a menu.
"I'm sure they didn't. I'll be back for your orders."

The menu was the same as it had been back
in 1912. "I don't even know what any of this stuff
is," Samantha noted as she read. "Consommé fer-
mier, fillets of brill, egg à L'Argenteuil."

"Try the roast beef sandwich," Jessica suggested. "At least we've heard of that."

Trevor returned with silverware wrapped in
white cloth napkins. "So how are you ladies liking
the cruise so far?" he asked.

"Trevor, tell us the truth. Does the crew inten-
tionally try to scare the passengers?" Samantha
asked. "Is that part of the so-called *fun*?"

"No!" he replied emphatically. "Not at all. We copy the *Titanic* as close as we can. But we would never purposely scare anyone."

"Are you sure?" Jessica pressed him.

"Really," Trevor insisted. "Why? Did something frighten you?"

Speaking rapidly, the girls poured out their stories to him. "And then when we saw that there were miniature replicas of us on that model ship, we got so creeped out that we had to leave," Samantha concluded.

"I can explain that," Trevor ventured. "The costumes you have are almost exact replicas of clothing worn by passengers. I don't remember anyone hired to dress as Astor, though."

"And what about the locket that's following me around?" Jessica challenged.

Folding his arms, Trevor studied them skeptically. "I think you two are trying to scare *me*."

"Honest, we're not," Samantha assured him. "It's all true."

"Let me put in the orders," Trevor said. "Give me a few minutes, and I'll show you something that might interest you."

In several minutes, Trevor returned with their drinks and a large album tucked under his arm. He laid it on the table between them. "This isn't the original, but it's an exact replica," he told them. "It might interest you while I'm getting your food."

The girls gazed down at the big hardcover album. In gold letters the words *White Star Cruise Line:* Titanic *Passenger Lists* were embossed.

Gently opening the ledger, Samantha read the first page. "Maiden voyage. April nineteen-twelve. Passenger list."

"When the voice spoke to me, it called me Alice," Samantha recalled. "It must think I'm Alice

Littlefield. Let's see if we can find her in here. It might tell us something."

The girls sat at the table, running their eyes up and down the columns, mesmerized by the seemingly endless list. All these people from every walk of life, rich and poor, thought they were taking the most wonderful journey of their lives on the greatest ship ever built. None could have dreamed of the tragedy about to befall them.

Samantha quickly saw that there would be no help in finding the maid's name here. "Astor, Mrs. J. J. and Maid," she read. "Aubert, Mrs. N. and Maid."

"Here's a Mrs. A. Fortune," Jessica said.

"That's her husband's initial." Samantha had realized that there were no first names listed for married women. "His name was probably Arthur or Albert or something like that."

"I'm seeing double!" A male voice spoke from behind them.

In unison, the girls turned. John stood between them.

"How did you find us?" Jessica asked, her voice becoming higher and more whispery, like it did every time she flirted with a cute boy.

"I thought I was only searching for one of you. Now I'm confused. Which one of you did I talk to yesterday?"

"Both of us," Samantha told him.

"We're sisters," Jessica added. "I never told you my name."

"I didn't realize." He pulled up a chair from a table behind and sat between them. "Ah, I see you're going over the passenger list. What are you looking for?"

At the same moment, each sister nudged her

chair a little closer to John. He was *so* cute! Samantha noticed the adoring way Jessica gazed at him and realized she had been doing the same.

Should she tell him about their bizarre encounters? Samantha decided not to and hoped Jessica wouldn't, either. It might sound so foolish. What would he think of them?"

"We're just looking at the passengers' names," Samantha said. "They have some cool old-fashioned names." She began reading down the list. "Cornelia, Elsie, Harriet, Gladys, Alice . . ."

Alice!

"Here it is!" Jessica said as she searched through the lists. "Matilda Littlefield and Alice Littlefield."

Samantha and Jessica stared at each other as they read the notations beside their names. "Cabin two-ninety-nine!" they both cried at the same time.

"Excuse me," John said, pushing back on his chair and rising. "I'll be right back."

"Okay," Samantha murmured, still staring down at the album. Was this why the numbers of their cabin kept changing?

Trevor came back with two plates containing roast beef sandwiches. "Now you really have me scared," he remarked as he set them on the table. "You two look like you've seen a ghost."

Samantha pointed to the room number listed for the Littlefield sisters. "Remember we told you about the way our room numbers keep switching from two-sixty-six to two-ninety-nine?" she reminded him. "Look at this listing!"

Trevor pushed back his hair as his eyes went wide. "That's so sketchy."

"Isn't it?" Jessica agreed.

"You girls need to talk to my mom," Trevor said. "She's amazing with stuff like this."

"We can't," Jessica replied. "Haven't you noticed that there's no cell reception?"

"Not a problem — she works here, too. I'll tell her what's going on and see what she thinks."

"Thanks!" Samantha said. She had the feeling that if they didn't get help soon . . . well, she was terrified of what might happen.

I WONDER WHY John never came back," Jessica mused as they walked back toward their cabin.

"He might have run into someone he knew," Samantha guessed.

"Probably."

"Maybe we should tell Mom and Dad about this," Samantha suggested. "I mean, some seriously weird stuff has been happening."

"Why ruin the cruise for them?" Jessica disagreed. "They wouldn't believe us, but they'd still worry that something was wrong."

"I suppose you're right. Why do you think that ghost maid called me Alice? I *need* to know more about Alice Littlefield," Samantha mused unhappily. "I feel like it's important."

They stopped in front of their cabin door. "Okay, it definitely says two-sixty-six, right?" Samantha said.

"Right," Jessica concurred.

They entered the cabin, both gazing around warily. Everything seemed to be as they'd left it.

Jessica sighed. "I *need* a shower. But I don't want to open the wardrobe for my robe. That locket is in there."

"No. You kicked it down the hall. Remember?" Samantha reminded her.

"You're right. Oh, good. Okay." Despite her words, she didn't open the wardrobe.

"What's wrong?" Samantha asked as she changed into her pajamas.

"What if it's back in there?"

The idea gave Samantha gooseflesh. She couldn't even tell her sister she was being crazy. Together, they stared at the wardrobe. Did they dare open it?

"I don't need my robe," Jessica decided.

Samantha nodded. "No. You don't really need it."

Jessica grabbed her nightshirt from her open suitcase and headed for the bathroom. "Oh, I forgot. No shower — only a tub. I wish they had *some* modern conveniences on this ship. Oh well." In the middle of the bathroom sat a claw-footed, gleaming white porcelain tub with ornate golden fixtures. A white lace shower curtain hung on an oval rod and could be drawn all the way around.

While Jessica ran the tub, Samantha tried to focus on the articles in Jessica's fashion magazine that predicted next season's must-have styles — anything to take her mind off recent events. She had to rest her brain. It was becoming exhausted from trying to figure out what could be causing all these strange happenings.

"Did you see how John was smiling at me?" Jessica called from the bathroom over the sound of the running faucet. "I'm pretty sure he likes me."

Samantha didn't want to argue. But Jessica just annoyed her so much sometimes. "He was smiling at me, too." Samantha couldn't resist countering. He *had* smiled at her, too. Just as much as at Jessica.

Jessica appeared in the bathroom doorway wrapped in a towel. "You?"

"Yes, me," Samantha confirmed, indignant at Jessica's disbelief. "I think it's me he likes." There! She'd said it, and she was proud she had. "It's not so impossible to believe."

"I didn't know you were even interested in boys," Jessica remarked skeptically.

"I like boys. Some boys," Samantha responded defensively. "Remember Robbie Alan last month? He called my cell almost every night for two weeks."

"Yeah, but *you* weren't interested in *him*."

"So? It still proves that a guy could like me."

Jessica folded her arms and narrowed her eyes, studying Samantha as though seeing her in a new, unfamiliar way. "You're still too young for John," Jessica decided confidently, turning back toward the bathroom. "He's at least fifteen — maybe even sixteen. Besides, he wasn't smiling at you."

"He was!"

"No, he — Oh, you're the sweetest sister. You're

just giving me a hard time to take my mind off the locket. Verrrry funny — saying he was smiling at you." Jessica shook her head. "I should have known you were kidding," she added, chuckling as she headed into the bathroom.

Furious, Samantha scooped the room-service menu off the bed stand and hurled the leather binder at her sister. It bounced off the bathroom door just as Jessica shut it behind her.

Jessica could be so conceited sometimes! It never even occurred to her that John might like Samantha more.

From behind the bathroom door, Jessica began singing a popular song. Normally Samantha liked her sister's singing. She had a good voice. Sometimes they sang together and Samantha enjoyed harmonizing.

"This is stupid," Samantha muttered softly. They were fighting over a boy who they barely knew. He hadn't said much in the café. They didn't even know anything about him. And then he'd taken off without saying good-bye.

He *was* good-looking, though. There was no denying that. When John looked at her, Samantha was sure there was something special between them. Maybe it was just the twinkling light in his blue eyes.

Still, she didn't want to fight with Jessica. In addition to being her sister, Jessica was also her best friend.

A celebrity interview in the magazine caught Samantha's interest, and she was soon caught up in it, forgetting her concerns for the moment. Mentally she was far away, but gradually she became aware of something thrashing around like a wild animal caught in a trap.

It was coming from the bathroom.

GETTING OFF the bed, Samantha approached the bathroom door. The faucet was still running, which made it difficult to hear. There was a ripping sound, as if cloth were being torn, and then a bang.

Pressing her ear to the door, she listened more closely. The thumping and thrashing kept up, and she detected something that sounded like muffled cries.

Samantha's heartbeat accelerated. This didn't sound good at all. Was some animal in there with Jessica? She remembered the scratching and whimpering.

"Jess? Jess, what's going on in there?"

No reply.

Something crashed against the wall. Glass shattered.

"Jess! Open the door! What's going on?"

Then a warm sensation caressed her toes. Her socks were wet.

Water was seeping under the door.

Samantha turned the doorknob. Locked! Frantically she shook the knob with all her strength. "Jess! Open up! Jess!"

She had to get help!

But she couldn't leave her sister in there!

"Help!" Samantha shouted, still shaking the knob. "Somebody! Help!"

A dark-haired woman ran in from the hallway. She was dressed in black pajamas, wrapped in a red-and-orange paisley-print satin robe. Her tumble of curls created a mane of dyed black hair around her lined face. "What's wrong?"

"I can't open the door. My sister's in trouble in there," Samantha explained, speaking fast.

"Ah! I knew it!" the woman exclaimed. Coming beside Samantha, she placed both of her palms on the door and leaned into it as though she were attempting to push down the door. "Spirit, depart!" she shouted.

Surprised, Samantha looked at the woman quizzically. What was she doing?

"Depart now, spirit! Spirit, depart! I command you to go!"

"Do you think that's really helping?" Samantha questioned doubtfully. They were wasting precious time. "Maybe I should wait here while you go get some —"

The woman ignored her. "Go! I command you, spirit! Go!"

Something within the lock snapped.

Samantha and the woman exchanged an anxious look. Had it opened?

Samantha tested the knob. Yes! Throwing the door back, Samantha and the woman rushed into the steam-clouded bathroom.

"Oh my gosh!" Samantha shouted as she slogged into water on the floor. Through the misty fog she could make out that the rod that had held the shower curtain now lay in the water and the curtain was bundled under the water of the overflowing tub.

"Jess!" Samantha shouted as she realized what she was seeing. Jessica was wrapped from head to

toe like a mummy in the white lace shower curtain, struggling blindly to free herself. She was
drowning in the tub.

"Help me!" Samantha shouted to the woman
who had come into the bathroom with her.

Jessica was sinking even lower below the surface
of the flowing water. It was as though an invisible
hand was pushing her down. Jessica's entire body
writhed as she struggled to get above the water.
In minutes she would lose the battle.

"Pull the rod away!" Samantha implored the
woman. The woman sprang to the tub and yanked
it away. Immediately the two of them hoisted
Jessica up so she wouldn't sink any deeper below
the water's surface. Samantha yanked the lace
curtain from Jessica's face, while the woman shut
off the faucet with a *clank*.

"Spirit! I command you! Depart!" the woman

shouted at the top of her voice, standing in the middle of the room with her arms outstretched. "Leave, I tell you! Leave!"

A fierce growl filled the steam-choked room.

"Go, I say!" The woman's tone held authority and strength. "Go, now!"

A calmness fell over the bathroom. Samantha felt the gooseflesh on her arms settle back into her skin.

Kneeling in the water, Samantha held on to her sister. Jessica didn't seem to realize that she was now safe. "Leave me alone!" she shouted. "Stop it! Stop!"

Samantha tightened her hold on Jessica to calm her. "It's okay! It's all right!" Slowly Jessica stopped waving her arms, and her hands flew to her face as if to block out the terror of what had just occurred.

"Something attacked me!" Jessica cried, terrified. "It grabbed me by the neck and shoved me down. Then it ripped the shower curtain off the hooks and wrapped me in it." She began to sob. "It kept holding me under the water. I was so frightened!"

"Let's get her into the other room," the woman advised.

Nodding, Samantha put a towel around Jessica's shoulders as they guided her to standing. Jessica began to rise but suddenly went rigid, her eyes going wide.

"What? What is it?" Samantha asked urgently. "What do you see?"

Jessica didn't reply but continued to stare at something. Samantha realized it was behind her and whirled around to look.

Words had appeared in the steam-covered

bathroom mirror. One after the other, they were drawn out by an invisible finger.

Slowly Samantha tried to make out the message. "Sta . . . stay . . . stay aw . . ."

Stay away! Or else!

T HE SPIRIT is still here," the woman murmured as they hurried out of the bathroom. "I have weakened it, but it has not fled. We must be very careful."

Samantha got Jessica seated on her bed and threw the covers over her to keep her warm. "I guess we'd better tell someone about the mess in the bathroom," Samantha considered. "We'll need to mop that up."

"No, we won't," the woman said, nodding toward the bathroom.

Samantha gasped. The bathroom was dry and the tub once more stood with the oval rod and lace curtain just as they had been, as if nothing at all had happened. Samantha looked to the woman for an explanation.

The woman rose and went to the cabin door, opening it. 266. "This said two-ninety-nine when I got here. It's changed."

"It's been changing back and forth since we boarded," Samantha explained.

"Trevor told me about what has been happening to you girls," the woman said. "He's my son, whom you met earlier."

"Do you believe us?" Jessica asked.

"Of course she does," Samantha said. "She saw the numbers change for herself."

The woman nodded thoughtfully. "I believe

that the number only says two-ninety-nine when we are in the presence of the supernatural. Since it is now two-sixty-six, it's safe to say the spirit has left. Rather, I should say, the spirits."

"There are more than one?" Samantha questioned.

"I sensed two in the bathroom. They are both gone now."

"I'm Samantha, and this is Jessica." Samantha introduced them. "What's your name?"

"My name is Rula Valenska. I am known to the ship crew as Madame Valenska."

"Thank you for helping us," Jessica said.

"I startled the spirit, breaking its concentration long enough for the door to open. I thought it had fled, but it was in there with us the whole time."

"Both spirits?" Samantha asked.

"No. The second spirit entered after we went into the bathroom."

"How did you get it to leave?" Samantha asked.

"I have been dealing with the spirit world for many years," Madame Valenska replied. "I've grown sensitive to the vibrational patterns that spirits emit. Over the course of time, I have trained my voice to vibrate at a frequency that frightens them." Sam recalled the richness and resonance of Madame Valenska's voice when she spoke to the spirits.

"It was lucky you were walking by when I called for help," Jessica remarked.

Madame Valenska shook her head ominously. "It was not luck. I came as soon as Trevor told me what was going on. Thank goodness I came when I did. Only a person as experienced with spirits as I am could have contained such an agitated spirit." She extended her arms majestically, which caused her many bangles to jingle.

Jessica and Samantha exchanged charged glances. What were they getting into? Was this woman for real?

A wry smile appeared on Madame Valenska's heavily lined face. "I am being honest with you. This unruly spirit is capable of real damage."

"Trevor told us you work on the ship. Are you a medium for the cruise line?" Samantha asked.

"Exactly! But I do not read palms or contact the dead for the entertainment of passengers. I work undercover."

"Undercover?" Jessica asked. And then, as though the words sounded appealing, she snuggled down beneath her blanket, laying her head on her pillow.

"Yes," Madame Valenska answered. "When the cruise line re-created the *Titanic*, a tsunami of souls from the spirit world landed on its deck. They were all former passengers from the *Titanic.* It was a golden opportunity for them. *Lots* of unfinished business to be resolved, it seems."

"Unfinished business?" Samantha questioned.

"Grievances left unvoiced, love words never spoken, apologies neglected — that sort of thing," Madame Valenska explained. "No one expected the *Titanic* to sink, after all. The passengers all assumed they had time to take care of those things in the future. Little did they suspect that there was no future for them."

"Wow," Jessica whispered. "Sad."

"Very sad," Madame Valenska agreed. "Though, most of the spirits on this cruise are benevolent enough. They are not out to hurt anyone. Some just want to finish the journey they set out to take. Others wish to see old friends again. They are here for many reasons. When the cruise line realized what was going on, they hired me to deal with it."

"What do you think this thing wants with us?" Jessica asked.

"I do not know. This is a very angry spirit," Madame Valenska said. "I have not encountered it before."

"It's a she. I saw her," Samantha told the medium. "She was in a maid's outfit and searching for a locket."

Jessica suddenly sat bolt upright and began screaming.

17

MADAME VALENSKA and Samantha leaped to standing, alarmed. "What happened?" Samantha demanded urgently.

"The locket's back!" Jessica shouted. "I slid my hand under the pillow just now to get comfortable, and I found it." Withdrawing the chain and locket from under the pillow, she held it out to them.

Samantha recoiled at the sight. Was she

imagining that the locket seemed to pulse like a living animal?

"Drop it, now!" Madame Valenska commanded.

Jessica tossed the locket to the floor. As if it was alive, the locket snaked its way under the bed.

Instantly Jessica was out of bed, standing. "Make it go away — for good," she begged Madame Valenska. "Can you?"

"Perhaps. I am not certain yet. When did you girls first encounter this locket?"

Speaking quickly with their words overlapping, the sisters told her how they had seen it in the Haunted Museum and how it seemed to have been following them ever since.

"The Haunted Museum," Madame Valenska repeated with a sigh. "I should have known."

"Known what?" Jessica asked.

Madame Valenska shook her head wearily. "That place is not what it seems. Did you touch the locket while you were in the museum?" Madame Valenska inquired.

The sisters looked at each other guiltily before nodding. "I just wanted to see the pictures inside it," Jessica confessed.

"And I only touched it for a second, just to shut it," Samantha put in.

"A second or an hour — it doesn't matter when it comes to the Haunted Museum — a touch is a touch," Madame Valenska said ominously.

Samantha's head snapped toward Jessica. "I told you not to touch it," she reminded her sister accusingly.

"Sorry," Jessica said sheepishly. "I couldn't help it."

"There were signs everywhere. *Do not touch!*"

"Yeah, but I didn't know it was haunted!" Jessica defended herself.

Samantha decided to let it drop. Laying blame on Jessica wasn't going to help things. "It doesn't matter," she gave in. "We both touched it."

Madame Valenska shook her head absently, clearly deep in thought. "That means you're both under its spell. This spirit wants more than only the locket. The locket is part of something greater."

"How can you be certain?" Jessica asked.

"My intuition," Madame Valenska replied. "The locket is what started the haunting, but it is more than the locket alone. Perhaps it is this particular cabin or even you girls yourselves."

"Us!?" Jessica gasped.

Nodding, Madame Valenska knelt on the floor and groped under the bed for the locket. Like something alive, it wriggled away from her grasp, snaking itself out from under the bed and twisting along the floor.

Squealing with horror, the sisters scurried to the closed door, pressing against it, ready to flee into the hall if it came toward them. Jessica turned her face against the door, too frightened to even look at the locket.

A deep and rhythmic hum began to emanate from somewhere deep in Madame Valenska's throat. Soon its buzzing vibrations of chantlike music filled the cabin.

The locket stopped whipping across the cabin and settled. It was like a cobra succumbing to the powers of a snake charmer. Without stopping her song, Madame Valenska stooped to pick up the locket, gripping it firmly with both hands.

Samantha turned away from the door to watch as Madame Valenska ran her fingernail in the seam between the two halves of the locket until it clicked open. Eagerly the girls flanked her on either side.

"It's me!" both sisters cried out at the same time.

In the locket, the vague, faded photos had grown clear. In the right-hand photograph was the back of a boy, turned away. In the left half were the photo portraits of two pretty girls with large brown eyes. Their abundant chestnut-colored hair was pulled up in flattering loose curls.

They were dressed in costumes identical to the ones Jessica and Samantha had worn.

"They must be Alice and Matilda," Samantha realized. "The Littlefield sisters."

"What should we do?" Jessica asked Madame Valenska. "We can't go through the whole cruise with these terrifying things happening. I'm scared."

Madame Valenska stood and pulled a pair of

narrow, purple-jeweled reading glasses from the pocket of her robe. Putting them on, she scrutinized the photographs in the open locket. "These two sisters might not be in the same photo," she observed. "The pictures might be laid on top of each other. The passing years and maybe even the time spent underwater could have fused them into one so that they look like they are together."

The sisters looked down at the locket, each one peering over one of Madame Valenska's shoulders. "There's a third person in the locket picture," Jessica observed softly. "Look."

Samantha saw it immediately as Jessica pointed to the blurred shadowy image of a girl behind the two Littlefield sisters. She glanced up sharply at Madame Valenska. "Could it be the ghost?" she asked.

Madame Valenska snapped the locket shut. "Possibly. Allow me to hold on to this," she requested. "It might draw the spirit to me instead of to you. I will be better able to handle whatever comes."

"Are you sure you can control it?" Samantha asked as she and Jessica jumped away in alarm.

Madame Valenska resumed her chant and nodded.

"Great idea, then!" Jessica agreed. "Take it with you. Definitely. I don't want it."

"All right," Madame Valenska told them, momentarily ceasing her chant. "I have a special box full of calming herbs that will hold it. From now on, I advise you girls to stay together as much as possible. I will mediate on what you have told and see what comes to me." She began to chant once more.

Samantha grabbed Jessica's hand and squeezed. "Thank you! We'll stay together — won't we, Jess?"

"Yes! Yes!" Jessica agreed eagerly. "Absolutely."

Without another word, Madame Valenska swept out of the cabin, still clutching the locket. Jessica and Samantha sat looking at each other, speechless. "Are you all right?" Samantha asked after a moment.

"Not really," Jessica replied. "It was horrible, Sam! I thought I was going to drown in that tub! Now I know how you must have felt down in steerage."

"Did the spirit say anything to you?" Samantha asked.

"She kept pushing my head under the water and each time when she let me up she'd sort of growl at me and say, 'I told you I'd get you!' over and over! 'I told you I'd get you!'"

Samantha nodded, remembering how scared she'd been when she'd heard the ghostly voice. "I know. It's really frightening."

Someone knocked on the door and the sisters grabbed each other's hands. Together, they moved to the front of the cabin. "Hello?" Jessica asked softly. "Who's there?"

18

JOHN."

Jessica threw open the door. "What's wrong?"

Samantha saw that John's skin was ashen. "Come in," she said, pulling him toward her. "You're freezing," she noted. "What happened?"

"Sorry to bother you," John apologized. "I didn't know where else to go."

"You're pale as a ghost," Jessica noticed.

"I don't know about that — but I think I've just *seen* a ghost," John told them.

"Was she in a maid's outfit?" Samantha asked him.

John's eyes went wide with surprise. "You've seen her, too?"

"I have!" Samantha confirmed. "Yesterday. Did she say anything?"

John placed the straight palm of his hand inches from his nose. Samantha noticed he was trembling. "She got right up to my face!" he cried in a quaking voice. "This close! And then she started screaming at me."

"Could you tell what she was saying?" Jessica asked.

He nodded his head. "She said, 'How could you?!' She kept shouting it over and over."

The girls told John about Madame Valenska.

"I've heard of her," he said. "Some of my friends on the ship have met her. They say she's amazing."

"She seemed pretty amazing to us," Jessica confirmed.

"We should go see her," Samantha suggested. "Maybe she can talk some sense into this spirit."

"I hope so," John said.

"All right. In the morning," Jessica said.

"Good idea," Samantha agreed.

"Thank you for believing me. Good night," John said, backing out of the room.

The girls said good night to him and sat looking at each other, exhausted. "I don't know about you, but I'm getting tired," Jessica said finally.

"Me too. But I'm too scared to sleep," Samantha admitted.

Jessica began shoving her bed closer to Samantha's. "Don't go anywhere, not even to the bathroom, without waking me up," she insisted.

"Not even to the bathroom," Samantha echoed. "Let's sleep with the lights on."

"I don't think I can."

Samantha knew this was true. Jessica always had to have complete darkness in order to fall asleep. "Try. Please?" Samantha coaxed. The idea of lying there in the dark was more than she could stand.

"Okay, I'll try," Jessica agreed reluctantly.

In bed, Samantha wrestled with her pillow until it was just right and settled down to sleep. In the bed close beside her, Jessica wiggled and thrashed as she struggled to fall asleep with the lights on, flipping onto one side and then the other. Normally Samantha might have complained about Jessica's fidgeting, but it was a comfort to know that her sister was there. With a wide yawn, Samantha nestled deeper under the blankets and managed to drift off.

When Samantha opened her eyes again, it was because she heard the scratching sound once more.

This time, though, it wasn't in the wall.

It was coming from the door. Something outside the cabin was trying to get in.

Glancing at her sister's bed, she saw that Jessica was all rolled up in her blankets and snoring lightly. Samantha longed to wake her but knew how difficult it had been for her to fall asleep in the first place, and so she let her continue sleeping. She wouldn't wake her up unless she truly needed to — and she really, *really* hoped she wouldn't need to.

Tossing back her covers, she sat up and listened. *Scratch scritch-scratch.* Whatever was making that sound was definitely out in the hallway.

Samantha pulled the sheets back over herself and sunk down under them. Every part of her wished the noise would simply stop. If she went back to sleep, she hoped it would be gone in the morning. It was better to stay here in bed — the nice, cozy, warm bed, where at least she *felt* safe.

Scratch scritch-scratch.

Scratch scritch-scratch.

Samantha covered her ears. *Stop it!* But the scratching kept on. What was out there? The sound was driving her crazy. How could she make it stop?

Finally it was more than Samantha could stand. She *had* to see what was there. Drawing in a deep breath to steady her nerves, she slid out of bed and crept noiselessly to the door.

Scratch scritch-scratch.

Slowly Samantha turned the knob.

She pulled the door toward her — just the very narrowest crack.

Peering out, she saw that no one was there.

Then a dog barked. It was right by her feet!

Samantha's eyes darted downward toward the sound. John Jacob Astor's dog, Kitty, stood in front of her. Upon seeing her, it panted and danced excitedly, shifting its weight on all four paws. Then it barked again.

Samantha squatted down to pet it. "Is it you who's been scratching all this time?" She suddenly felt foolish for being so frightened by the sound. "Are you lost? Your owner is searching for you."

The dog yipped, looking up at her. "What is it?" she asked. "Are you trying to tell me something?"

The dog replied with another high-pitched yip. Samantha expected people to start coming out of their cabins to complain about the barking.

She turned sharply, staring back into her cabin. "What's wrong?"

Kitty jumped up on the open door, scratching and barking at something just above Samantha's head. Turning, she looked at the door number. 299!

She drew a sharp breath. "Two-ninety-nine," she breathed.

Did the dog know what it meant? Was it trying to warn her?

Samantha turned sharply, and her eyes darted around the cabin. "Who's here?" she called softly. "Go away!"

Samantha realized the barking had stopped and looked for Kitty. But the dog had disappeared.

Stepping into the hall, she looked in one direction and then quickly in the other. There was no sight of Kitty and no nearby hallway she might have turned down.

How had Kitty disappeared so quickly?

19

Samantha stared at the numbers on the door and made a decision. Tomorrow morning, they were getting out of this cabin. Even if they had to sleep on the floor of their parents' room, it would be worth it for all the strange encounters with maids and necklaces to be over.

Returning to her cabin, Samantha crawled beneath her covers. Jessica was still sleeping heavily, but Samantha vowed to stay awake until dawn to keep watch. Despite her fear, though, exhaustion soon overcame her and her eyes drifted shut.

Restless dreams started right away, and in her sleep Samantha ran down an endless corridor of the ship, pursued by shrieking passengers who fled a rushing wave behind them. Just as the water was about to overtake them all, Samantha's eyes snapped open.

Someone was shaking her arm.

The room was dark and she was staring up into Jessica's moonlit face. Samantha shook her head, struggling to come awake. "What's going on?"

"Come with me," Jessica said. "I have to show you something."

"Where are we going?" Why were the lights off?

"Come on," Jessica insisted, taking hold of Samantha's hand.

"Your hand is ice-cold," Samantha said.

"Just come on," Jessica repeated.

"Wait, Jess, I want to get dressed."

"There's no time. Let's go."

"All right," Samantha agreed. Swinging her legs out of bed, she allowed her sister to pull her toward the door. Holding it open, she stepped out into the hallway. "Wait, Jess! My feet are really cold." Looking back inside the cabin, she used the light from the hall to help her search for flip-flops, sneakers, or even socks to warm her feet.

What she saw in the cabin made her breath catch in her throat.

Jessica was still in her bed! The covers rose and fell in time with the familiar, steady rhythms of her breath.

If that was Jessica . . . who was standing beside her?

Suddenly icy with fear, Samantha whirled toward her companion and stared into the nearly colorless eyes of the ghost maid.

A scream froze in Samantha's throat as, with lightning speed, the ghost maid clamped a viselike grip around it, choking off any sound. The hallway spun and the last sight Samantha saw were the numbers *299* on the cabin door before she fell backward into blackness.

• • •

The next thing Samantha knew, she was standing on the Grand Staircase leading down into the first-class lounge. Looking up, she gazed at the huge, illuminated glass dome ceiling above. In front of her, ornately carved wooden railings encased spiraling ironwork that flanked both sides of the staircase leading into the ballroom. At the beginning and end of each railing were carved pineapples. In the center, a third, beautiful wooden railing cut the staircase into a right and left entrance and ended with a carved wooden cherub that held an illuminated electric torch. A ticking noise made Samantha turn to look at an elegant clock set into more carved paneling. It was the most gorgeous place Samantha had ever seen.

Still dressed in her pajamas and with bare feet, she felt completely out of place gazing at the richly dressed people below her who glided across the dance floor to the music of a waltz.

Was she dreaming? That had to be it! *Wake up! You're in a dream. Wake up!*

It didn't work. She bit hard on her thumb to check. *Ow!* The pain was real enough.

How had she gotten there?

Remembering, she looked around sharply for the ghost maid but didn't see her. Well, that was a relief, at least.

Turning to leave, Samantha spied a door to the right of the stairway. When she went to pull the handle, though, it was locked. Trying the door on the other side of the stairway, she discovered that she couldn't open it, either.

A tall, severe-looking butler appeared. "Follow me, Miss Littlefield," he said somberly.

Miss Littlefield?

"How did you . . ." Samantha's voice trailed off as the butler proceeded down the stairs ahead of her. Did the staff here really know who everyone was supposed to be? She didn't have a name tag or anything. How could he possibly have known she had been assigned the passenger Alice Littlefield?

Hurrying down the steps, she caught up with the butler, grabbing his sleeve to stop him. "Excuse me, but I really just need to get out of here and —"

"Why would you want to miss this lovely ball?"

"You can see that I'm not dressed for —" Samantha stopped herself as she realized that she now wore a gleaming sapphire-blue evening gown that swirled to the floor. Her hair was swept up elegantly on the top of her head — and the silver locket was around her throat.

Samantha's hands flew to it.

No!

How had this happened? Trembling, Samantha fumbled with the clasp, but her hands were shaking so badly that she couldn't grasp it. "Please," she begged, turning her back to the butler. "Help me get this off. Please!"

The butler shook his head and raised his palms defensively. "There's no reason to take off that lovely locket. It looks elegant on you. Rest assured that you're perfectly dressed, miss," the butler insisted.

"I just want this locket off!" Samantha wailed as she trailed him on his way down the rest of the stairs.

"You look lovely," the butler insisted as he disappeared around the dancers.

The classical music swelled as the dancers spun around the immense dance floor, moving together as one. It would have been breathtaking had she not been so confused and frightened. Not knowing what else to do, Samantha found an ornately carved golden chair with red velvet cushioning and sat to calm her racing pulse.

"Caviar, miss?" A waitress dressed in a black dress under a white apron offered the contents of her tray.

Samantha had never tried fish eggs, and she wasn't going to pick this moment to be adventurous. "No, thank you," she declined.

The waitress leaned in closer. "Sally Kelly is out to get you tonight. You'd best be careful," she hissed her warning.

"Sally Kelly?" Samantha questioned.

With a subtle tilt of her head, the waitress gestured toward a spot across the room. The ghost maid stood glaring at Samantha with hate-filled eyes.

"Why?" Samantha asked the waitress.

The waitress laughed scornfully. "You don't know?"

"But I don't!" Samantha told the waitress. "Please, tell me."

The waitress laughed again as she moved away. "I'm sure you know exactly why."

Where was Sally Kelly now? Samantha's eyes darted around the room searching for her. Was she gone? Samantha decided she had to get as far away as possible from the spot where she'd last spied the ghost maid. To do that, she'd have to cut across the dance floor.

Samantha entered the densely packed dance floor, stumbling among the serenely swirling dancers. They bumped into her, indifferent to her presence, caught up in the dance. One man stepped on her hem, and Samantha heard it tear.

Wake up! she commanded herself. *Get out of this dream now!*

Samantha weaved and dodged blindly through the crowd. If she stayed within the dancers, Sally Kelly might not find her. But where was the ghost maid? Samantha worked her way toward the sidelines of the dancing crowd, straining to locate the ghost maid. Suddenly she tripped over the feet of a man in a tuxedo. Her arms windmilling, she fought to keep her balance but crashed into the back of another maid with a tray who stood off to the side of the dance floor. Small tea sandwiches slid across the floor as her tray clattered to the ground.

When the maid looked down at Samantha, it was Sally Kelly, her hate-filled eyes burning. "This is no dream, Alice Littlefield," she snarled. "No dream at all!"

Samantha bolted up and ran back into the crowd, hoping to escape this horrible creature. There had to be a way to escape, but for now, all she could hope to do was hide.

20

Samantha pressed up against a pillar at the back of the dance floor, trying to make herself as small and unnoticeable as possible. She had lost sight of Sally Kelly, but it didn't make her feel much better. That creature might pop up again when she least expected her.

As she caught her breath, she took the time to work once more on removing the locket from her neck. To her delight, the clasp opened easily. Filled with horror at the thing, she bent forward and flung the locket along the floor. Hopefully the dancers would crush it beneath their feet.

Something licked Samantha's hand. Startled, she pulled it back, but a second look made her smile. "Kitty!" she cried, delighted. Descending into a squat position, she drew the dog to her. "You're freezing," she noted, ruffling her tightly coiled fur to warm it. "Have you found your owners? They must be here somewhere."

Kitty yelped in response and Samantha laid her hand over the dog's muzzle to quiet it. She didn't want to attract attention to herself. "Sh-sh," she soothed. "How did you get so cold? Were you out on deck?"

Kitty barked sharply, panting with agitation. Following the dog's gaze, Samantha saw Sally Kelly heading in her direction. Samantha wasn't sure if the ghostly creature had spied her yet, but she would very shortly if Samantha didn't leave this hiding spot and find another.

"I've got to go, Kitty," Samantha said urgently, releasing the Airedale from her grasp as she stood. At any second, Sally Kelly would see her.

Before Samantha could move, though, someone tapped her sharply on her shoulder. It was John, dressed in a tuxedo. "You dropped this, I think," he said, presenting her with the locket.

"I don't want it. Throw it away!" Samantha said in a breathless whisper.

He unclasped the two sides. This time the photos were clear. On one side was a picture of John — and on the other was Samantha's picture.

"Then I *am* the one you like," Samantha said with a quiet smile, gazing happily up at him.

"It's always been you," he confirmed. "Let me hold this for you," he suggested, dropping the locket into his pocket. "Might I have the favor of this dance, Miss Littlefield?"

All the fear and terror was washed away at once as Samantha basked in the warmth of his tender smile. How handsome he was! What beautiful eyes! As he put his arms around her waist, she melted into him and marveled at his strength.

Samantha had learned the basics of a waltz in gym class and did her best to stay in step with her partner. Effortlessly spinning away in John's arms might be the perfect way to make her escape unnoticed. Hopefully he could also tell her something that might help her figure out what was going on. "Why did you call me Miss Littlefield just before?" Samantha asked as they glided across the ballroom dance floor.

"Surely everyone here knows Alice Littlefield."

"They do?" Samantha asked, surprised. "Why?"

"You and your sister are so charming and beautiful."

"Wait! Are you talking about Jess and me or about Alice Littlefield and her sister?"

Before John could reply, a terrible cracking arose and he pulled her close. "It's that time again," John whispered ominously in her ear.

A line of broken wood shot across the dance floor like jagged lightning. Looking down, Samantha saw the planks rip apart, revealing the room below them.

What was happening? Samantha looked back at John for his reaction and gasped, her entire body going rigid with shock.

Half of John's face had turned a putrid green, his teeth yellow and rotted. One of his eyes was red-rimmed and bulging; the other was out of its socket entirely. His skull peeked through the place where a patch of scalp had come off.

"It's that time again," he repeated, blowing foul breath into her face.

Samantha broke free from his grip. Turning in a circle of horrified amazement, she saw that the once elegant group of dancing passengers had now *all* become grotesque rotting corpses like her dance partner. They continued to dance, but the waltz was now sped up. Despite the accelerated tempo, the decaying dancers dragged each other across the dance floor in slow motion.

Samantha held her head as the room began to spin. Gathering up her gown, she staggered toward the Grand Staircase. The door out remained locked but, just the same, she strained on the crystal knob with all her strength.

The butler pulled himself up the Grand Staircase. His uniform now seemed frayed and torn, his flesh rotted. "I'm afraid you're not permitted to leave, Miss Littlefield. No one can."

The ship abruptly lurched to one side. Samantha was thrown onto the stairway's iron rail just as the door cracked off its hinges. Rushing through the opening, Samantha tossed away her low-heeled pumps and raced barefoot into the darkened hallways, running desperately.

It didn't seem that anyone was following, but Samantha didn't slow down until she finally found her way back to room 266.

266! She heaved a sigh of relief, happy that she'd left the door open since she had no key.

Opening the door, she took a second reassuring glance at the numbers. 266 meant she was safe. And then — as she smiled up at the numbers . . . they jumped.

299!

As if an invisible hand was pushing her, Samantha stumbled into the dark room. The door slammed shut, and immediately the lock clicked, the double bolt sliding into the locked position.

"Who's there?" Samantha shouted. "Who is in here with us?"

No one answered. Samantha turned to her sister's bed. The moon shone from the porthole onto the rumpled empty blankets. Jessica wasn't in her bed!

"Jess! Jess!" Samantha called in the darkness.

Jessica suddenly appeared in the bathroom doorway.

Samantha rushed to Jessica, hugging her. "The most horrible thing just happened," she cried. "It wasn't a dream, either. Look, I'm still in this strange dress."

The urge to get out of her strange old-fashioned garb was suddenly overpowering, and Samantha began pulling it off. "It was so scary, Jess. I don't even know how I got there, but the ghost maid —

her name is Sally Kelly — she fooled me into thinking she was you."

Jessica continued to stare.

"The place was full of zombie creatures and I was trapped in there with them." Samantha kept up her frantic pace. "And the locket came back. But listen, we have to get out of this cabin now. Something pushed me inside the room and now the numbers say two-ninety-nine. You know that's not good!"

Samantha was so happy to see Jessica. Scared though she was, having her sister with her was a big comfort.

"Oh, and wait until I tell you about —"

Samantha cut her sentence short, studying her sister curiously. Jessica wasn't responding to her at all. Her sister only stood there stiffly. "Jess? What's wrong?"

21

JESSICA WORE an elaborate white ruffled night-gown. Where had she gotten *that*? Samantha knew she hadn't brought it, and the wardrobe department had been closed for the evening.

Her sister's face was a blank, as if she were walking in her sleep, although that wasn't a thing she'd ever done before this cruise.

"I know what you did," Jessica said.

"What are you talking about? Of course you do. I just told you what happened."

"You snuck out to be with *him*," Jessica snarled.

"Who?"

"John!"

"No, I didn't," Samantha protested. "Listen to me. This is more important. There's something I have to tell you about John."

Jessica stepped into the room and faced Samantha squarely. Illuminated by the moon, her face was twisted with anger. "You love him, don't you? Admit it!" Jessica commanded.

"Have you lost your mind?" Samantha asked. If this was a joke, Jessica's timing couldn't be worse. "Are you kidding me? Don't even go near John!"

Jessica slapped Samantha forcefully across the face.

Stunned, Samantha staggered back, covering her stinging cheek with her hand. "What was that for?" she demanded, furious. Her sister had never before laid a hand on her.

"You know very well what for," Jessica answered in a strange, stiff, accusing tone. "John loves *me*. He would never be interested in a little nothing like *you*."

Folding her arms, Jessica turned her back on Samantha. With her face still stinging, Samantha stared at her sister's back — only this wasn't her sister. She was completely changed. Had some spirit taken her over while she slept?

Tears jumped to Samantha's eyes. Exhaustion and terror gripped her. Why was this happening? Was she loosing *her* mind?

"I'm going to him now!" Jessica cried. She reached into her nightgown and withdrew the locket.

"How did you get that?!" Samantha asked, shocked to see the locket again.

"John gave it to me!" Jessica opened it and revealed the pictures inside. On one side was John and on the other was Jessica.

"But the locket should have a picture of John and me inside," Samantha insisted. "I saw it myself."

"You're insane with jealousy," Jessica accused Samantha. "This locket shows me and him. Meet us on deck. Let him tell you himself that he loves me."

With a click, the door unlocked itself and swung open, as if an invisible force was assisting Jessica in her departure. Samantha watched her leave, stunned. When Jessica was in the hall, the door slammed shut with a bang that rattled the cabin.

With her hand to her cheek, Samantha soothed her burning skin. She couldn't be mad at Jessica, though. Some terrifying possession had overwhelmed her. Whoever that was, it wasn't Samantha's sister speaking.

And then the reality hit her. Some*thing* had Jessica. That something was taking Jessica to John right now. Handsome, charming John who was not at *all* what he seemed to be. She pictured his rotted corpse of a face close to her own and shuddered.

The closest clothing Samantha could find was the beaded maroon shift Jessica had left draped over a chair. Quickly she tossed it on and slipped into flip-flops. She had to go help her sister.

22

As SAMANTHA stepped out on B Deck, she saw John and Jessica right away. They stood in the moonlight holding hands. Jessica saw Samantha coming toward her and a smug, triumphant smile spread across her face. It said: *You're too late. It's me he loves.*

"Get away from him," Samantha warned, working to keep her voice calm and steady.

Jessica smirked. "I don't think so. You're the one who needs to go away."

"Jess, he's not safe!"

"What did you just call me?"

"You're my sister, Jessica."

A suspicious expression formed on Jessica's face. "I'm your sister, but you know my name isn't Jessica."

Samantha studied the girl she'd assumed was her sister. Outwardly she looked the same but something wasn't right: her eyes were cold; the set of her mouth was cruel. The Jessica Samantha had always known never wore an expression like this.

"If your name isn't Jessica, what is it then?" Samantha asked cautiously.

"Matilda, of course. Matilda Littlefield. You know that, Alice."

The air stirred beside Samantha, reminding her of a whirlpool, and she ducked out of the way. Slowly an image took form and Samantha saw her own double emerge from the churning atmosphere. She was dressed in the same beaded frock, but unlike Samantha, who was now disheveled and in flip-flops, this girl was perfectly put together: her hair plume neatly pinned, her boots laced and tied, and her silver locket hanging at her neck.

Alice Littlefield eyed Samantha and then stepped toward her. "No," Samantha screamed as the ghost stared her in the eyes. "No!"

It was no use. There was nothing Samantha could do to stop the spirit from stepping into her body.

We're one now, a voice in Samantha's head spoke. *I have taken you over. You are me now. You're Alice.*

Inwardly Samantha rebelled, struggling to hold on to herself. "No, I'm Samantha," she muttered. A young woman laughed inside Samantha's head, a light self-assured sound.

The force of Alice Littlefield's possession was too much for Samantha. It felt like an overpowering fatigue that she could no longer fight. She couldn't control her movements or her mind.

John spread his arms wide. "Don't worry, girls. I love you both. You can share me."

"Share you?!" the sisters spoke in one voice.

"Why not?" John asked.

"Absolutely not!" Matilda shouted.

"Never!" Alice confirmed. "Never in a million years!"

Matilda lunged at her sister, pulling her hair and screaming names at her. She raked Alice's cheek with her nails, drawing blood. Alice fought back with equal ferocity, kicking and biting.

She gripped her sister's shoulders and tossed her back against the railing. To escape her, Matilda backed up onto some crates that had been piled there. Alice climbed up after her, but the two sisters froze as the sound of barking filled the air.

A pack of nearly twenty dogs — poodles, terriers, cocker spaniels, beagles, dachshunds, and boxers — rounded the corner. In their midst was John Jacob Astor, his lanky legs taking long determined strides. "You'd better get to the lifeboats," he informed them. "This ship is taking on water. Women and children first."

"That's right, we're sinking!" a woman echoed.

Both sisters turned to see who had spoken. It was Sally Kelly, the ghost maid. "Many will die," she said, eyeing the sisters malevolently as she walked up to them. "But you girls are going first."

With tremendous strength, she flipped Matilda into the air, knocking her over the railing. "Don't you upper-class snobs make a play for my John," she shouted. "He's *my* man!"

The slumbering Samantha overthrew Alice Littlefield's hold on her as she saw her sister fly backward over the rail.

In a flash, Samantha grabbed for her sister. "Got you!" she shouted, her fingers wrapping around Jessica's wrist.

"Alice!" Matilda screamed as she dangled over the side of the ship. The only thing saving her from the churning, frigid black water below was her sister's determined grip on her wrist as Samantha balanced precariously on the stack of crates.

"You're next, dearie," Sally Kelly threatened as she began climbing up the boxes toward Samantha. The ghost maid grabbed Samantha's leg, preparing to shove her up and over.

Still holding tight to her sister, Samantha

looked back into Sally Kelly's cold eyes. "Let me go!" she demanded. "Let go!"

Suddenly Sally Kelly's voice rang out with surprise and pain. Kitty had jumped up behind her and grabbed the back of her maid's uniform, dragging her backward. The ghost maid fell onto the deck as Kitty jumped on her, pinning her to the ground.

Samantha turned back to her sister. "Hang on to me. I'll pull you up."

"But we both want John!" Matilda cried out.

Samantha felt Alice Littlefield reawaken inside her. *Drop her*, she urged Samantha. *That's what I did. I let her go so I could have John to myself.*

"I know you're going to drop me — so do it now!" Matilda shouted, crying.

"Go away, Alice Littlefield!" Samantha shouted. "Alice Littlefield, get away from me!"

"Just do it!" Matilda wailed.

"You're my sister, you idiot!" Samantha replied as she clapped on to her wrist with both hands. As Jessica began to rise, Samantha used every bit of her strength to hoist her sister up high enough so that she could grip the railing and pull herself the rest of the way up.

Together they fell backward onto the deck. Looking up, Samantha saw the ghosts of the original Alice and Matilda Littlefield still struggling on the crates. Kitty barked as Sally Kelly managed to get away and join the ghostly battle.

"Jealous, petty spirits of the *Titanic*, be gone!" Madame Valenska stood on deck, her paisley robe fluttering in the wind, her arms raised high. "Spirits with evil intent, depart! Depart this ship!"

The ship lurched to one side. Samantha and Jessica slid as everything around them tumbled past. They banged into a wall, shielding their faces from flying debris.

Madame Valenska clung to the railing. Her curls whirled around her head as she shouted into the wind. "Spirit of Alice Littlefield, depart! Spirit of Matilda Littlefield, depart!"

The Littlefield sisters were enveloped in a spinning funnel of silver wind. They began to decompose and then disappear altogether.

"Spirit of Sally Kelly! Depart!"

Sally Kelly crumbled into dust, which a vortex of wind scattered into the air.

"John Teller, depart!"

John fell to his knees, contorting in pain as a spirit arose from him, a near look-alike, and then flew apart into the night like sparks from a camp-fire. John immediately crumpled to the deck, passed out.

With a bark, Kitty ran off down the deck, until she turned a corner and vanished out of sight. Watching her go, Samantha realized that the ship was no longer tilted but once again level.

"You saved us," Samantha cried as Madame Valenska came toward them.

"Thank you!" Jessica said. "Thank you so much."

Standing, she hurled the locket over the railing with all the strength she possessed.

"Samantha not only saved you both, she saved Sally and John as well," Madame Valenska remarked. "You should be proud of yourself."

Samantha smiled. "I couldn't have done it without you, Madame Valenska."

"How did you know we needed you?" Jessica asked.

Madame Valenska smiled as Kitty came trotting back toward them. "A little doggy told me," she said as Kitty disappeared into thin air right before their eyes.

"Wow!" Samantha murmured.

"Did that ghost dog really tip you off?" Jessica questioned Madame Valenska.

"Indirectly she did," Madame Valenska confirmed. "It was Kitty who led Trevor to the newspaper article that helped me figure out what was going on."

23

THE NEXT morning, Jessica and Samantha sat in the first-class café where they'd first met Trevor. Madame Valenska sat with them, savoring her cup of tea. It was the time between breakfast and lunch, so there was only one other couple at another table and Trevor was able to join them.

Jessica turned to Trevor. "It was a good thing you found that article tucked away in the passenger list that night."

"I know," Trevor agreed. "It must have fallen out when I showed you the list. After you left, a cute little Airedale trotted into the café. She kept barking until I followed her to the article on the floor. It was like she wanted me to find it."

Madame Valenska took the folded article from her pocket and set it on the table. "I read this as soon as Trevor gave it to me: 'Untold Tale of the *Titanic*' was the title. It's quite a story," she reported. "The article tells about a little-known incident on the *Titanic*. On April twelfth, just two days before the ship sank, two sisters fell in love with the same boy. He was a boiler worker named John Teller.

"John Teller worked on ocean liners and would sweet-talk the rich female passengers. All the while, though, he was really engaged to one Sally Kelly, who followed him from ship to ship working as a maid.

"While on the *Titanic*, John made a play for the Littlefield sisters, figuring if he couldn't catch the interest and money of one sister, he'd have the other's fortune.

"He took the locket he'd given to Sally Kelly and put the photo of Matilda Littlefield over Sally's photo. Then he stole it back from Matilda, telling her she must have lost it, and gave the same locket to Alice, with *her* picture inside. He told her to keep it a secret, claiming they would marry when they arrived in New York. But Matilda realized Alice had the locket and accused her of stealing it.

"Meanwhile, Sally Kelly learned that one of the sisters had her locket and she wanted it back!"

"I don't blame her!" Jessica interjected.

"What a rat," Samantha added.

Madame Valenska stopped and stretched. "I agree," she said. "And it gets worse."

"What happened?" Samantha asked.

"The two sisters struggled over the locket on the *Titanic*'s deck," Madame Valenska went on. "Sally Kelly was fed up with her fiancé's ways and got into the fight. In the end, the sisters went overboard together, and Sally and John knocked each other into the ocean, as well."

"Now that's what I call unfinished business," Jessica remarked, picking at her corned ox tongue, one of the many unfamiliar old-fashioned specialties of the café.

Madame Valenska nodded. "I happened to come in for a late supper and Trevor showed the article to me. I was beginning to put it all together and this confirmed my suspicions."

"We can thank Kitty for pointing it out to me," Trevor added.

"Good old Kitty," Samantha said fondly. "I was so scared of that scratching, but the sweet dog was looking out for us all along. It's too bad Kitty was a ghost. I miss the little pup."

"I wouldn't be surprised if the dog shows up now and then," Madame Valenska suggested. "Obviously Kitty was very fond of you girls and isn't the sort of spirit that would hurt anyone."

Just then, John came in with a pretty blond girl and took a table with her. He waved to the girls when he noticed them, and they returned the greeting. Trevor got up to go take his order.

"Here's something I don't understand," Samantha said. "How did he get mixed up in this?"

"The same way you did," Madame Valenska explained. "You told me you both touched the locket in the Haunted Museum. When they say not to touch anything in that museum, they are not kidding around."

"I don't think he would touch a locket," Jessica said.

"Well, he touched something," Madame Valenska insisted.

"He *was* in the Haunted Museum when we were," Samantha recalled. She remembered how interested he was in the model of the *Titanic*. Perhaps he hadn't been able to resist touching the one they had in the museum.

"Do you think he's even that cute?" Jessica asked Samantha.

Samantha studied him. "He's all right, I suppose." At the moment she couldn't remember what she'd thought was so enchanting about him. But maybe that's what it had been — an enchantment, a sort of spell.

"Maybe it was his name that connected him," Trevor suggested. "Both are named John Teller, aren't they?"

Madame Valenska nodded in agreement. "The spirit world is mysterious."

"Thanks again for your help, Madame Valenska," Jessica said.

"Samantha saved you. When she refused to turn on her sister, she broke the spell of the locket. All I did was clean up. Those spirits would have had no more hold over you without the power of the haunted locket."

Samantha picked up the article Madame Valenska had placed on the table and unfolded it. Inside was a photo of Sally Kelly and John Teller. Both were smiling and Sally wore a wedding dress. She read the headline: UNTOLD TALE OF THE *TITANIC*. It was the same article, but as she perused it, the story being told was completely different. It told of John Teller and Sally Kelly, who were married on the *Titanic* and were very happily in love.

Samantha passed the article around the table for all of them to see. "Are you sure this is the same article you read last night? Are we still being haunted?" she asked Madame Valenska nervously.

Madame Valenska considered the question for a minute before answering. "I don't think so. I believe this has happened because you have changed the past. By breaking the locket's spell and staying loyal to each other, you created a world where the story of John Teller and Sally Kelly could have a different, happier ending."

"Amazing," Trevor commented.

"Totally," Samantha agreed.

"You know," Jessica said. "There's a Haunted Museum not far from the dock in New York."

"Aw, come on, Jess," Samantha wailed. "Haven't you had enough?"

Jessica sat back in her chair and grinned. "It was pretty exciting. I don't know if a person can ever have enough of the Haunted Museum."